OLD FIRES

Josh Patrick Sheridan

APRIL GLOAMING

This book is a work of fiction. Names, characters, places, and incidents are the product of the author's imagination or are used fictitiously. Any resemblance to actual events, locales, or persons, living or dead, is coincidental.

-First Edition

Publisher's Cataloguing-in-Publication Data

Sheridan, Josh Patrick
Old fires / written by Josh Patrick Sheridan
ISBN: 978-1-953932-07-5

1. Fiction - General I. Title II. Author

Library of Congress Control Number: 2021941488

For Penelope

Sunrise

IN THE MORNING TIM PUTS ON HIS HAT AND BOOTS and steps out into the great blue valley. He crosses muddy tire tracks in the yard with a pair of slender chickens at his heels and sets a grocery bag on the hood of the Ford and takes out several bottles of cleaner and a roll of paper towels. He sprays the truck's dash and the handrails, using extra where blood has pooled and thickened, scrubs until the entire cab is clean. The bundled quilt, thrown in despair that night into the truckbed, ends up in the trash. A handmade gift from his mother, his favorite since boyhood. Behind him the fog lays on his back like a sleepy child.

The sheep's pen is in back of the barn. They are hungry, braying maniacs. He dumps a bucket of feed into their trough. There you go, he says. Shhh, there you go, and he unlocks the gate and lets it swing open and walks away.

Inside he sorts the dishes from the drying rack into cabinets. Grace has left the radio playing on the table beside the couch, where it could sing to her while she dozed. She kept it low enough that he wouldn't have to hear it, but now, six days later, the house is so quiet it might as well be blaring. He shuts it off. In the cellar he twists off the water supply and gathers the crabapples from Grace's bin in his shirt and takes them out to the horse. John, she'd named him. Old Man John. Always Grace's horse with the graying mane and the long, beautiful face. He unties the rope on John's paddock and nickers with his cheek and the old fellow steps out into a wide open world. Ten feet. Twenty. Then around and back inside, a long-toothed inmate afraid of his parole.

He calls the electric company, the telephone company, the water company, the man who delivers firewood, the man who delivers hay.

He puts the heelers in the bed of the Ford and drives a mile over the ridge. The nearest neighbors in a double-wide, their domain of scrubland and limestone. The dogs jump down and follow him through a graveyard of plastic toys and rusted garden tools. Two brothers, their bare bellies pressed against the screen door, suck at fingertips and watch the dogs. When their daddy comes they disappear into the house.

The boys' habit of going shirtless has been acquired honestly.

I hate to see this, Len Surbaugh says, coming onto the stoop. He pinches the filter from a cigarette and drops it in the yard.

The boys'll feed these dogs?

Take good care of them, Len says, rubbing absentmindedly at the patch of hair on his chest. Them boys love dogs.

Tim hands him the bunched leads and peels a twenty from a small wad in his pocket. Get you started on food.

Len fits his smoke between his lips and takes the bill.

They ain't pets, Tim says. You gotta take them out.

Len holds the bill up. We'll take them.

They need work.

We know how to keep a dog.

The heelers are sniffing at a firepit full of folded beer cartons. One of them lifts his leg to it.

Well, Tim says. Thank your boys for me.

Like I say, Len Surbaugh says, leaning to tuck the bill into his pocket. I hate to see this.

⚜ ⚜ ⚜

John stands at the gap in his paddock as though the gate is still closed. Scattered crabapples at his feet. Tim bends and chooses one and holds it out and John closes his lips around it and crunches. One more, Tim says. And then, One more. The horse might be smiling. When the pile is gone he scratches John's chin and goes inside.

He takes the folded duffel from a closet shelf and opens it on their bed. There are still crumbs of French mud inside. His dad never the cleanest man. He goes to the bathroom for his soap, razor, toothbrush, comb, deodorant. He tucks them into the side of the duffel. He finds a book, a flashlight. Some photographs and a shirt that might be the one Grace was wearing the day they found out she was sick. He puts them in. Five pair each of socks, underwear. Three t-shirts. An extra pair of jeans. The bag is maybe a quarter full. He takes the bread and peanut butter from a cabinet and cans of beer from the refrigerator, wraps them in clothes and puts them in. His small cardboard box of tobacco makings. Finally, the Colt 1911, also from Europe, later come through Vietnam, his dad's initials cut into the barrel.

He stands and looks at the near-empty mouth of the duffel and sighs. The bag is simply too big. There is no way to fill it.

They lived their married lives on seventeen acres in a cut of the Alleghenies settled originally by her grandparents. The cornerstone of the house still read the year, 1922, chiseled in sandstone and steady under the weight. The homestead passed along to the kids for nothing but the fees to make it legal.

The old folks had kept sheep, a pair of milking cows, a stall of pigs. Grace had been in love with the land as a child and loved it all the more once it became hers: the blueberry patch wild enough to be a nuisance, the trees on the creekbank that whispered at night. A great flat stone over the water from which she skinny-dipped in the evening, lips chattering, skin puckered and blueish. Her stiff hair slick against her back. Tim would throw her towel over a high branch as a joke and she would use him instead, his shirt, his big body, to dry.

Up a rolling hill, a track in the pale dirt to softer grass and a shade tree. The first place they'd gone on their first day of living there.

Was it anything like this, she'd asked, always wanting to know about Asia.

He'd sworn he wouldn't lie to her. Fill the whole of it in with trees, he'd said, and give them leaves as broad as a man's back. Make them thick enough that you can't see anything past one but the trunk of the other. Also, the day can't be this beautiful. You have to picture constant rain. The noise of it. How hard it is to walk through all the mud it makes. The smell of sweat and dirt and shit on men's bodies.

OLD FIRES

She leaned into him. So, nothing like this, she said.

The sun came through the leaves of the shade tree and scattered stars on the grass at their feet.

If this place reminded me in any way of that place, he said, we wouldn't be here. It was an absurd thing to say: everywhere reminded him of Vietnam. The simple fact of living reminded him that for just over a year he might as well have been dead.

Still. Their seventeen acres was enough for some semblance of happiness. There were fish to catch, a garden to tend. Pasture enough for the hens. The four sheep were unnecessary holdovers, sons of bitches that refused to die. But they kept to their paddock and didn't mind cheap feed, so he never got around to giving them the bolt.

The Ford coughs and turns over and the radio snaps on. He can't remember what he'd listened to after the hospital or why he'd have listened to anything. The doctor using the word *gone* in place of the word *dead. She's gone, she's gone now, I'm sorry, Tim, but she's gone.*

Turns out the echo of a bullshit word lasts longer.

He'd driven to her parents' house and stayed with them until after the funeral, slept on the couch beneath a painting of the Crucifixion. Eaten their potatoes. Drank too much of her father's jug wine.

Their driveway is a mile and a half of rut. The shifting of minor glaciers has left behind wild divots, and the Ford wheezes and whines, bouncing up and down like a carnival ride. In the past he's made a game of steering recklessly between these hazards, but this morning he does not bother. He keeps straight. He drives too fast. Outside, the freshly-budded tree branches swell and lift; they reach for him like desperate people, dig with their fingernails, make terrible wailing sounds against the paint. A family of deer in the neighbor's field comes to attention as though someone has fired a gun. They watch him carefully. He is nothing to them, but at a moment's notice he could become everything. They seem to know this.

There is a rough spot where the driveway joins the main road. The place where two worlds—modernity, call it, and heritage—run into each other, imperfectly paved, banked at an odd angle, crumby with loose asphalt and road litter. A place of farmer's philosophy, of lightweight moral reckoning. He frequently pauses here for traffic, and in those moments he thinks he can see the exact spot where the two worlds are met. To turn onto the main road is to pass through a door in a mountainside and find yourself standing at the bottom of the sea.

❦ ❦ ❦

What if I come with you, he'd said.

It had been a good day, a day of strength for them both. The sun still early to set, the cold wind still chattering against the house, drawn toward the fire in a room Grace gleefully called the *parlor*. They were setting the table for dinner. A ridiculous thing: it was only the two of them. Still, he insisted on it.

Of course you're coming with me, she'd said. You'll have to drive me. A silk scarf around her head. Her pale, bloodless face.

That's not what I mean.

Dahling, she said, her best Vivien Leigh. *Whatever do you mean?*

You know, he said. When you go, I go.

They did not know it, but this was just weeks before the end. Just weeks before they were both alone in their unfamiliar worlds. They knew by then treatment hadn't taken, but couldn't fathom what that meant.

That's not funny, she said.

I'm not kidding.

Grace sat down, suddenly breathing more heavily.

You've been thinking about this?

I haven't stopped thinking about it since the first time it came to mind.

They'd been married three years and seven months. Grace had turned twenty-five the day before Christmas.

There's more to this life than just me, she'd said, but they both knew this was untrue. There was nothing more to life than what they'd built together. I trust you, she said finally. I trust that you won't do what you're saying.

What if I wait for you? What if I wait for you to give me the signal?

The *signal*?

That's it. What if you give me a sign. He was hopeful.

What the *fuck* are you talking about?

❦ ❦ ❦

He turns left, though right would do just as well. Stops at a convenience store for gas and coffee. The boy behind the counter someone he recognizes, someone from an old crew, maybe.

Jesus, Tim, the boy says.

Thank you.

Jesus, I think we all heard at the same time.

Thanks, I know.

Do you need anything? I dunno. Anything?

Ten in diesel. And a cup of coffee, Tim says. He holds out a twenty.

Just take it, the boy says, waving off the money.

Tim stands for a minute with the money hanging between them, then slips it back into his pocket. Nice of you, he says.

The boy smiles and leans in, like a conspirator. My girlfriend's been blowing my stepbrother while I'm here. They don't know I know, but of course I fuckin know. Her best friend told me. He glances to the side as though anyone else is interested in his story, as though anyone else is even around. Then he straightens. All that's to say, I know what it's like to want to get out of this fuckin town.

Right, Tim says. Sure, you get it.

Milk

HIS FATHER'S DUFFEL SHIFTS AND RUSTLES on the bench seat like a sleeping passenger. He glances at it now and then, the way one might if he'd seen a flash through the window and thought it a ghost.

Ahead of him the blue-green shoulders of mountains, their peaks in the sky like a movie about a ruined world. He is weaving, accelerating, the Ford's tight brakes catching on corners, the cold coffee in his styrofoam cup slurping up the sides and bubbling out the mouth. Springtime pollen collects in the windshield corners, white like snow.

The terrain has changed. He is out of the holler and driving across an alien moon; he feels it in the pressure in his ears and hears it in the shrill cries of hawks: birds that tend not to hunt in the deeper forest, birds that prefer open air and taller trees. The civilization sparse, a sideways town here and there, never more than a service station and a few houses, their skirts muddied knee-high with runoff from the winter thaw.

It's been several hours since he's thought about much of anything. The mountains hold that strange power: though there is much to see, much to intuit, none of it will be as you'd intended. He doesn't know if beauty is the right word but it isn't the wrong one, either. For him, these mountains are days of scrambling over chestnut logs, small fires, abundant game, pleasant people where there are people and lunatics where there generally are not.

He rolls the window down farther and lets the air rush into the cab. It smells like peat and rain. There is not a cloud in the sky.

Years ago, still kids, he and his brother Anthony had a bad habit of disappearing. Entire weekends. Illegal campsites. This was before the war, to which his brother had gone the year before him—though both had been in the jungle at once, and both had come home more or less alive. This was before then, before their mother's hysteria, before it became impossible to vanish without saying where to. The two of them in the truck, a carton of beer, a sack of McDonald's between Tim's feet. Cigarettes. Rifles. Tim remembers a dusty porno mag, possibly procured at a gas station. This may be apocryphal.

Anthony had an incredible laugh, clear and obnoxious, an embarrassment at movies but a signal flare in a crowd. Tim can still hear it, even through the wind, and remembers his brother laughing this laugh and turning sharply onto a road called Sand Lick Pike. A beer warming between his thighs and Hank Williams on the radio.

Where we going? Tim had asked.

Couldn't say, Anthony said. Never been here before.

Most times everything was fine. The wild country so big they could camp and be gone days before a landowner stumbled on their cold fire. Once or twice someone found them out, but no one ever ran them off. People understood the impulse they were chasing, had chased it themselves in their dreams, in their younger days.

They'd driven two or three miles and stopped at the place where Sand Lick Pike tapered into dirt. Parked on the shoulder and wandered into the woods, cleared a spot for the tent with their boots and drank themselves stupid. Their lives not yet anything, they talked about nothing for hours: their mother, girls, the towering tree fort they'd been constructing for years in the woods behind their mother's house. Their voices waterfalling down the steep sides of the mountain. He remembers a fitful sleep that night, boozy and cramped, and what might have been the hazy crackle of voices in the trees—advancing, retreating, advancing again, like swells of the ocean. Words that were not words. Ghost translations. Gibberish. His brother sleeping against him, back-to-back, their t-shirts sweaty and clung together.

In the morning the truck was still there, and for that they were thankful. He never mentioned what he'd heard.

On the leather curtain of the gear shift, a smear of blood he'd missed in cleaning up. He licks his thumb and wipes at it and, having nothing to clean himself with, licks his thumb again.

Grace's dreams became wild, aggressive things. She would shake the entire bed with her convulsing, scoot it several inches across the floor, snap upright panting and wide-eyed as though she'd witnessed the Second Coming. She would take a glass of water in one shot and together they would stand and rearrange the bedsheets and lie again beside each other.

Comfort was impossible on those nights. Tim with terrible nightmares of his own. Still, he tried.

A new one, he'd say.

A new one.

What was it this time?

One night it would be the slow draw of a blade from fingertip to elbow. Another, a frigid walk through a cornfield. Wolves. Rats. Crows with their sharp beaks at her eyes. Tim unable to tell her about his own solitary dream, of the skin melting off a little boy's back and falling like poured water into the dirt.

I'm so sorry, he'd say.

There will be morning again, she'd always tell him. For that, let's choose to be grateful.

There was much Grace chose to be grateful for. More and more, they were the things about life he hated the most.

He stops for lunch at a small white house wedged between the road and a mountainside. One of those places where the owner lives out back. The board on the porch announces grilled cheese and cobbler and it suits him fine.

A half dozen customers is enough to make the restaurant seem full. He does what others have done and removes his coat, drapes it reverently on the back of his folding chair, eyes the other patrons who are so clearly eying him. Most return to their plates, nickering their disapprovals. Everyone knows an outsider. But a slender young man, a boy really, alone at the next table, looks at Tim for a long time. The skin around his eyes is baggy and ashen. He picks something from between his teeth and makes a show of eating it.

You want peaches, he says.

Sorry, Tim says.

Peaches. From a can. Stay just as good all year round.

You mean in the pie? Tim says.

The boy turns in his seat to face him.

You going camping, ain't you? Got a bag in the truck, broke-in pair of boots. He points to the window beside Tim's head. So you going camping.

That's right, Tim says. Such as it were.

Then you want peaches. I got more peaches than I know what to do with.

Jonas, leave the man alone, someone says, and a girl comes from behind the flimsy wall between the kitchen and dining room. She is young and comely, full, beautiful by any measure in blue jeans and a clean apron. She works her hair into a ponytail and squeezes in behind the boy's table, lays her hands on his shoulders. He trying to sell you some peaches?

I'm not really sure what he wants, Tim says. He watches Jonas digging at something inside his nose. The girl pops him on the shoulder with her fist.

My Jonas ain't all there, she says, and looks at the boy with great care. He likes canned peaches a lot, so he buys too many every time we send him to the grocery store. Then he wanders around trying to sell the extra.

I turn a good profit, Jonas says. He flicks his head as though shaking away a fly. Be surprised.

I'm not really in the market, Tim says.

Nobody's ever in the market, are they, Jonas, the girl says.

The boy tilts his head to look at her. She is too young to have a child his age but touches him like he's hers. He seems ready to cry. Sons of bitches, he says.

I know, Jonas, she says, winking at Tim. Sons of bitches is right.

❧ ❧ ❧

The night before Grace went into the hospital, he'd somehow managed to fall asleep. The room hot and the air stiff as though someone had built a fire on the rug. She was curled into a ball beside him. He could feel her cold feet on his knees. She was breathing, which he'd promised himself he wouldn't take for granted. Still, he closed his eyes and drifted, and soon enough he was camping with Anthony again. The air in the tent a thousand pounds, the buzzing of insects outside loud as chainsaws. Anthony was snoring. Then, voices: faded, at first, as though spoken into pillows; then closer, ricocheting from trees. He made out many—a dozen, a hundred. When they closed around the tent, they shouted in celebration, he could hear their feet shuffling on the forest floor, the snapping twigs and static whisk of dead leaves, and then the tent was shaking, they were slicing at it with blades and reaching their pink fingers through the slivers—

He woke to Grace sitting upright, sobbing. Her fingers in her nose and blood running past her wrists.

I tried to wake you, she was saying. I tried to wake you! I tried to wake you! Where were you?

❧ ❧ ❧

Lunch is what he'd expected, a flat sandwich cooked carelessly on a hotplate, and afterward he stands smoking on the porch, watching the beginnings of the rain the earlier wind had promised. Tapping on the leaves like Morse code, pings on the hoods of lunchgoers' cars. The sweet, earthy smell of wet pavement. A good storm will give the mountains reason to breathe. The sky rewards the land with its water, the land rewards the sky with its air. As simple as it gets. The only circle that ever really mattered, and the only one that ever really will.

He feels someone behind him, knows it's the girl from inside.

Where you headed, Peaches, she says. Her voice smooth and thick as milk. She sits on the bench by the door and lights a cigarette of her own. The black name tag on her blouse says LeighAnn.

Couldn't say, he says. Never been around here before.

Never?

Never.

She is one of those nervous smokers who don't seem to know if smoking's really what they intended to be doing.

Well, she says, there ain't much to do, really. Eat more grilled cheese sandwiches. Drink liquor. Sit in the back yard and keep an eye out for Bigfoot.

I have the day ahead of me, he says. I guess I'll see what I see and stop when it gets along closer to dark.

She cocks her head. You running?

Well, he says. Yes and no. I ain't in trouble. I'm not that kind of running.

I get you, she says. I get you.

He looks at her for a second. Her eyeshadow is dark and imperfect. Her lips glossy. A smudge of mud, or chocolate, on her cheek. She doesn't seem to need him to say anything else.

She stubs half a cigarette on the heel of her shoe and stands. Well, mister, she says. Welcome to Sand Lick. I'm sorry to inform you you've now seen everything there is to see. Stop by for a sandwich on your way back around.

Through the window, he notices Jonas looking at him. The boy stares for a second, then cracks a horrible, blue-gummed smile.

Sand Lick, he thinks, driving away. *Welcome to Sand Lick*. And then: *Sand Lick Pike*. You've now seen all there is to see.

Paradise

THEY HAD NOTHING, REALLY, and the house was no exception. Stained wood floors. Greasy sink basins. The wallpaper yellow and faded, its glue would warm in the sun and cast dark spots along the hallway. When Grace worked the water in the kitchen the first time, it flowed brown and gritty. Her grandfather too old and too stubborn for maintenance.

It's all the same as it ever was, she said. Nothing's changed.

Tim found work on a paint crew in the town of Victory. The job simple and good and the pay fair. The shop owner, a man named Gus, was kind, boisterous in the way some heavy drinkers are. He kept malt liquor in his thermos and because of it, made other men climb the ladders. They never spent a moment feeling sorry for him. Simply laughed at his nature and did as he asked them to do.

Grace made money here and there substituting at Victory's small elementary school. Her passion for children only grew.

Slowly, slowly, the house began to shine again. When they got a few dollars, they scraped the old paint and replaced it, sanded the floors and re-stained them, repaired the fixtures they could manage. Grace had a game of dancing in the parlor in her socks, watching the overhead light flicker and spark on the hardwood. They left the windows open so the sun could warm them in the daytime, split the old folks' leftover firewood for the stove at night.

Evening darkness in the cut was total. Nights when he would come home late, down the long drive, and see Grace standing in the shadow of the porchlight, he'd ask if she could hear him that far away, worried that something needed fixing on the truck: a belt, a joint. No, she'd say, smiling. I could just feel you getting closer.

For others the living might have been a frustration, if not a downright hardship, but for Tim and Grace it was paradise: to do a little better each day than the day before, to love a little harder, to sleep a minute longer at night, to measure the corn against their knees, against their belts, against their necks.

❦ ❦ ❦

The storm is massive. The afternoon sky gone near-black, the trees wicked teeth in a gaping mouth. Rain on the windshield as though he's driving the center of a river. Here and there a cutoff but no road. Gaps in the trees like caverns; the muddy tracks borne through them could be driveways to hell. He sits with his shoulderblades pinched together and his hands closed at the top of the wheel. The music snapped off. The rain beating on the hood of the Ford like a husband desperate to get in.

Now and then there is a tug at his brain as though he's someplace he's been before, though the absence of recognition is still so godawfully total. Memory would never be so perfect, anyway; it would never be the trees but the smell of the trees; it would never be the road but the whine of the road. To realize he's been here feels both reckless and true. It can't be and yet it is. The wipers swipe, swipe, swipe, swipe, swipe, and then, in a second between them, the small green sign, its reflected edges, the hole in its corner possibly from a rifle shot, stuck in the mud in the middle of nowhere at the head of a road called Sand Lick Pike.

❦ ❦ ❦

Dean Goodell, a boy in the jungle, adapted to the darkness by going feral. He was from Charlottesville, educated at the university there, a degree in marketing or something. Sharp boy. He'd once told Tim he hadn't split for Canada because his mother told him not to and he answered to no higher authority.

They all became strange, but Goodell became animal. While the rest of them carried tablets to ward off jungle disease, Goodell pulled fish from the river barehanded and tore bites from them, heartbeat and all, believing their flesh had powers. He walked in formation with shimmering scales caked into his beard. He claimed to be sleeping while he walked, and they were inclined to believe him; once a mortar landed five yards from his right boot, close enough to soak his shins with groundwater. The line had instinctively crumpled away from the trail. Everyone except Goodell, who kept walking—ten, fifteen yards—who hadn't known what happened until they told him later that night.

Zip ordnance, Lieutenant Sizemore said. You and all these other fucks should be spray on my pantlegs.

Nope, nope, didn't see it, Goodell said. You're sure?

Of course I'm sure, cocksucker, Sizemore said. I was so sure I shit in my pants.

Didn't see it, Goodell said.

He'd adapted the ability to sleepwalk so he could stay awake at night and roam. Sizemore tolerated it as a matter of survival: Goodell had some devil's energy inside him that could only be burned off in the blackness of the jungle. They didn't know or want to know what he did, not really, though when a group of them found a forest deer one morning with its head snapped around backward and green flies eating at a hole in its carcass, they assumed it had been Goodell's handiwork.

Well. Some men took balled-up panties from their pockets at night and smelled them. Some wrote shitty poetry. Some, like Dean Goodell, slid between the trees with the stain of basa innards on their cheeks and wandered outside of humanity for a while.

Once he makes the turn he remembers everything. The pressure in the air. The rumple of the road and the tree limbs bending across it at protective angles, their leaves giving a little shelter from the rain. A few minutes and he can see the wide spot where Anthony had once parked their truck. Somewhere out there the bones of their campsite lay in rot, their beer cans and the ashes of their dinner, the hole they'd dug to shit in. He doesn't stop. The road turns to stone and, a hundred yards later, to dirt.

He wonders what would happen if he told his brother he'd found it again. Anthony might not even remember. This place holds no special meaning for him. Nothing spiritual. It's a cheap motel room. The toilet and the trash. He has to remind himself that Anthony had not heard anyone talking that night, had not heard the choir of voices ripping at Tim's ribcage. Amazing, in a way, that two brothers should experience a place so differently. The one waking and stumbling away and groaning at his hot piss on the frost, the other entirely too afraid to move.

The truck's nose seems pointed to the sky. He is too distracted to hear it struggling. After another mile or so, he passes a hand-painted sign: Calvary Church of Jesus With Signs Following. Pastor Dennis W. McIntire. Sunday. Wednesday. 2 Miles.

A wonder that the road should have two more miles in it, that he wouldn't sooner tumble off the edge of the earth.

For a while Grace's mother refused to visit. She was desperately afraid of her past, had been to the cut only once in fifteen years, the day they moved her father out. It had been so bad then, she'd said. The smell unbelievable. The dishes not washed in weeks. Mice ate crusty food from the table as though they'd been trained. She'd gotten a thick splinter in the meat of her hand looking under the couch for her father's billfold. The floors rough beneath the couch and smooth along her dad's old trails to the kitchen, to the bathroom.

After that day, she said, I wanted nothing to do with the place. I thought we'd sell it. I was going to give you the money.

But Grace had seen something there, something *more*, the potential to create in her own image. She looked at the curving banister and saw majesty. She looked at the iron cookstove and smelled cornbread. She'd known as a teenager the color palette it needed, and her opinion had never wavered. A hanging plant here, a piece of rug there. One day, maybe, they could re-do the bathroom upstairs, a nice floral idea, but she could suffer its ugliness until the money flowed more freely.

I'm glad you didn't get to sell it, she'd told her mother and father. Tim sitting beside her in her parents' stiff dining room, a room designed to help her mother forget her roots. His toes working into the plush white carpet.

Everything in Grace's parents' house so white he was nervous to act, to drink, to chew, to walk from one corner to the other lest his ass bump something irreplaceable from a shelf. The smell of the rooms like new plastic. Even the ferns whose stiff branches hung from the mantle were fake.

I love it there, he said, maybe out of turn and though it wasn't yet true. Though it was *close* to true: he loved that Grace was there, and that counted for something.

Her mother smiling sideways. I'm so glad, she said.

You'd be amazed how much work he's done, Grace said.

Her father quiet all night. Drinking vodka sodas. Tim stole glances, wondered if the farmhouse had once been *his* dream, too. A more lovable man than he chose that night to let on.

Finally, they did come. Her father's Oldsmobile going easy down the drive, her mother stepping out in ridiculous knee-high galoshes. They brought a six-pack of Coors and a bouquet of wildflowers. Tim left the beer on the porch to cool. When her mother stepped in, she reddened as though someone had slapped her.

Oh, she said. Oh, my God.

Tim smiled stupidly.

Oh, my God, her mother said again. Sweet girl, look what you've done.

❦ ❦ ❦

The Ford's engine quits with the whimpering sound of a vacuum cleaner cutting off. He's managed the good fortune of a relatively level spot, but that's all the fortune he's managed. The rain clamors down through the trees, a million people clapping, and a chill flicks across his neck like the tongue of a snake. A short ways ahead what might be a driveway. He slots the car into neutral and jumps out to push. It is slow going; the mud track of Sand Lick Pike is washing away layer by layer. An accidental river cuts down a gully on the side of the road. He digs the toes of his boots in and shoves. The truck a fat, dumb animal to be prodded. After maybe an hour, the daylight starting to fade behind the mountains, he manages to work her onto the driveway. Stops to collect himself, catch his breath. Down the path there is nothing to see, a dark tunnel into the woods that could be the open mouth of a whale.

He pops the hood and stands for a minute, listening to the hiss of wind over the engine's carcass. He dangles his flashlight over the parts, but nothing is out of place, nothing smoking. He knows without knowing that his fuel pump has failed.

He gets back into the cab and watches the rain wash down the windshield. Takes the 1911 from the seat beside him and looks at it: the times it served his father, the holes it put in beer cans. His acceptance of life's result not necessarily absolute; he can't really believe what he's convinced himself he has to believe. To force this thing into his mouth. To push it against his temple and squeeze. It will be brutal, but at least it will be immediate. Then again, he has no real idea about such things. He puts the barrel to his nose and smells it, its oil and age. The rain tumbles harder. Now is not the time, but it feels like the time. Slowly, he puts the end of the barrel between his teeth and clamps down, careful to keep his finger away from the trigger. The pistol tastes strongly, the pungency of pepper. Somewhere close lightning strikes and the resultant thunder is like a rifle snap directly behind him and he jumps and slides the 1911 away and lets it fall back to the bench.

When he steps outside again, his body is wobbly. It's difficult to get a good purchase in the softening mud.

Okay, he says, and pats the hood of the Ford. I'll be back. He hunkers into the neck of his jacket and starts walking. Immediately, intensely, he remembers the smell of these woods, as though their campfire were still burning, the eternal flame from a decade ago sending the whirling ashes of fast-food packaging skyward. He remembers the clamorous sound of the jungle, the cackling monkeys, the roar of explosions real and imagined; and here, this jungle, this dense forest, so relatively still. Calm, almost. Easy to see why Anthony had found it soothing enough to sleep through. He turns back once and is surprised that the Ford is no longer visible; without his permission, night has come full on.

Around a long bend the driveway narrows, becomes more claustrophobic. He wrenches himself deeper into his jacket. The far horizon, past the clouds, is aflame. While a man walks through the deep blue sea, the edges of the world burn with the sun's dying effort. The view is beautiful and intimidating.

He hardly notices that the rain has stopped. And then, as if sprouted from the storm's damp earth, just where the sun has winked out, the disgruntled black outline of a building.

Ghost

HE STOOD IN FRONT OF EVERYONE and opened a wire-bound notebook and laid it flat on the podium.

You should have known her like I did, he said.

They all looked at him, disarmed, having expected his voice not to work, having expected him to gurgle out a cough and sit back down. To whisper that he was sorry and step away. It's what they would have done had they been him. None volunteered to eulogize because none would have made it through. They were not him. They had not loved her the same. They had not loved her in the way it takes to open a mouth and allow another's life to pass through.

If you'd known her like I did, you'd have been amazed.

He took his time. Watched carefully as his fingertips trembled on the edges of the notebook. The feeling he had not of sorrow but of rage.

Sometimes the things she said were terrifying, he said. She believed so much in the beauty of people, in some kind of goodness in the world, and I had to explain to her how wrong she was. I didn't want her to get hurt, you know. I had to tell her there's no real goodness in the world, that it's only a passing feeling. All of it. Love, kindness, hope, happiness. Then one day she looked at me and said if what I told her was true then she must be looking at a ghost because I was the kindest man she'd ever met.

He locked eyes with Grace's father then, briefly, and saw no disagreement.

It scares me to say it, Tim said, and glanced at Grace's casket, at her folded arms and phony smile, but she was right. About everything. There is kindness in the world. Plenty of it. There is kindness in the world, but I can't see it, because I'm a ghost.

The house sags on its hips under years of dead wet leaves. Its back against a crumbling wall of shale. In the purple light he can see that some of the windows are blown out, that the stoop has come separated. An overgrown trail in the yard that leads over the side of the hill and into the depths of nowhere.

He approaches carefully: the soft squish of mud beneath his boots, the natural groan of the world turning. He squeezes between the stoop and the door and knocks, thinks how surprising it would be for anyone inside to receive a visitor. No one comes. How stupid to hope for a phone; there are no wires to the house. The place is not connected to anything. An island in the woods.

He climbs the stoop and leans against the trailer to look in a window. Enough light still to fill the places where people might once have been. The window looks in on the kitchen: a kettle turned on its side; cabinets flung open, empty; a stack of newspapers on the counter. What kind of strange end this place must have met. What kind of violence.

It was Goodell that roasted the Vietnamese boy. A crossroads in the mountains west of Da Nang, eleven men who no longer recognized themselves, a place that was not home and therefore did not operate under the rules of home. Goodell furious, barking, his beard dripping with spit, roasting people's houses, roasting the grass at his feet, roasting trees and the dogs trying to hide behind the trees. Tim could not remember if he himself had fired on anyone that day, but he could remember coming around the side of a hut and seeing the drenched back of Goodell's hair, his body turning on an axis, torching the entire world, and then, for a split second, Goodell stopped, and the boy flew out of a doorway, running barefoot toward the jungle, and Goodell pulled his trigger and roasted him.

Who wants Q, Goodell kept saying, Who wants Q, under his breath, like a mantra.

That day had not been normal, but the day before had been, relatively so, and the next day was, and the weeks that followed were the same as they usually were—boring and anxious and wet and lonely—and after a while anyone who saw what Goodell had done forgot about it in the stink of war. Tim was in America before he thought of the boy again, and already his mind had changed things about him: his mind gave the boy a thicker shock of facial hair, put a gun in his hands, made angry sounds come from his mouth when he left his hut. His imagination bent time and aimed the boy's gun at Goodell and gave the crazy bastard no other option but to roast him.

They shook him and the parts of him. His hands. His body. Their voices shook his insides. They made their solemn ways from platter to platter, this and that to eat, greedy mouths too full to speak. They hugged him and left crumbs on his shoulders.

What a tragic world, they said. Some variation of it.

So young and beautiful, they said. Sometimes they said *lovely*. Sometimes they said *vibrant*. They were all saying the same nothing, their lips moving differently and the words more recognizable or less depending on the type of food they were eating. The women were breathy and smelled of wet powder, and they towed their men behind them, men who had become adept at pretending to choke on emotion.

Grace's mother had flickered in and out of the room. Her mouth open for no reason and her hand at her throat, like a haunt.

He tries the knob but it's locked, so he pops one of the plastic panes out with his fist and reaches in and undoes it from the inside. The door swings open and an unholy smell rolls out, a tide of filth and neglect.

Hello, he calls. The mouldering carpet drinks his voice up.

He steps in and covers his mouth and nose with his shirt. There is a sofa on the rear wall, a television resting on its face on the floor. Its cord stretched across to an outlet. The smell is of plant life, the natural world taking over, of wet mushrooms, dogs caught in the rain. The living and dining areas one room, a small bathroom, a small bedroom. The extent of it. He opens a slender closet and in the dying light finds a dry bar of soap, a hand towel that smells of rust, a stack of bent, worked-over photographs. In a kitchen cabinet a sock of pennies and a paper bag of baseball cards, soft with use. The life savings of a small boy. He shifts his weight and comes down on something hard. A ball of buckshot in the flesh of his hand. He looks up at the wall, at moonlight pouring in through a thousand tiny holes above the stove.

⚜ ⚜ ⚜

Grace believed her grandmother lived in the house with them. She swore up and down that the kitchen still smelled of Sunday dinner, that there were times when she'd come upstairs just in time to hear the sink stop running. Her grandmother had left her favorite rocking chair in the parlor and it would sometimes start up, back and forth, back and forth. Grace told him the old lady must still enjoy the radio, and when he asked why, she said some days, when she woke early, she'd come downstairs and it would be on.

Her grandmother had been good mountain folk. Knowing in the ways of tincture and snakebite, of scrap cuisine, of teaching a dog to sing. Grace relayed family stories of corn shuckings and barn dances. The day such and such got his finger cut off only to have it regrow, boneless and flicking, like a salamander's tail. The day the beautiful farm girl fell in love with the scarecrow and was embarrassed that night by her partner's terrible dancing. Hill country stories of questionable truth and flexible morals. Still, there was something comfortable in their patterns, how the downtrodden and ignorant always managed, in the end, to find some sort of supernatural restitution.

If only that was real life, he'd said one night, after Grace finished telling the story of Punkin Steeple, the local giant who'd vanished into a coal mine and resurfaced fifteen years later a senseless midget afraid of the sun.

It *is* real life, she replied. Granny Lea knew the boy with the lizard's tail for a finger. He lived around here.

Tim set his fork down on the edge of his plate and looked at her. Why do you always insist, he said.

Grace smiled and finished chewing. Oh, love, I'm just way ahead of you is all, she'd said. One day you, too, will begin to insist.

* * *

He humps the loose duffel down the path gone pitch-black, a breeze chilling the sweat on his neck. It seems a bad idea, this, but then there are times when the bad idea and the only idea are one and the same.

In the bedroom of the trailer he finds a limp mattress and drags it to the living room. Sets the TV onto the chair. Its face shattered, tiny pieces of glass woven through the carpet. He sits on the mattress, fixes a peanut butter sandwich, eats it in three bites, fixes another. Then he cracks one of the warm beers and gulps half down. He is weary. His boots tight around his swollen feet. There have been hundreds of nights that he would have been happy for this shelter, nights when he could not remember what home felt like, but now it is black and awful, folding, squeezing. Collapsing, like a lung.

He pulls the flashlight from the bag and leans into the photographs from the closet.

* * *

Some days the Vietnamese boy joined him wherever he was, as though they were father and son. Riding shotgun in the truck, standing quietly in rooms and watching Tim paint, sitting cross-legged in a buggy at the grocery store. The more Tim saw him the more he realized how beautiful he'd been: his big black eyes, his slick hair, the strong jawline of his ancestors. The boy had a peculiar build, the awkwardness of a prideful teenager willing his jangly body to stand straight, to do as he'd seen his heroes do. They never spoke because there was nothing to say. The boy never asked him why he hadn't shot Goodell in the back of the head.

Tim didn't tell Grace about him, about the eyes or the teeth or the ribbons of skin that fell from the boy's body when he moved. She would have told him he was insisting, and he would have had to tell her she was right.

There is a party. Maybe fifty people in the yard of a shabby building, some gathered around picnic tables, the children barefoot and chasing. A group of men clustered at the treeline with cigarettes at their mouths, their shirts outdated but crisp. Overweight women with casseroles, dresses with pastel flowers, long ponytails. A lean man sits on the stoop, his head cocked toward these women as though directing them; hair cropped close, the ankles of his pants riding high up the leg. In another picture the same man is front and center at the base of the steps, the flock spreading away from him like wings. He is smiling and so are they. He's wearing thick black glasses like the ones the army issues. They make him look insane.

And there, off to the side, barefoot in a long dress, the girl from the restaurant, the one with the sandy hair and the lean walk who'd gently beaten the peach salesman away. In the picture she is younger, meek-looking, crooked and pale in the sun with her eyes cast to the side. As though she's no interest in having her photograph made. As though she's just noticed a snake winding through the yard.

Water

HE WAKES IN THE DEAD OF NIGHT with his clothes on and a terrible thirst that reminds him he hasn't brought any water. He rifles through the duffel and comes out with a can of beer and finishes it without taking it from his mouth. He finds the last one in the bag and does the same. He can smell the mattress he's fallen asleep on: his body heat warming the reminders of its previous occupants, their sweat and odors and dandruff, the spread of death sinking into the fiber. Suddenly reeling, he stumbles onto the stoop and pukes into the yard. When he is finished, he wipes his mouth with the back of his wrist and retches and pukes again. He looks back through the door and inside the trailer and is struck with a twisting pang of disgust. That he'd slept here. That he'd eaten here. That he'd ever entered here at all.

The moon is spread across the yard and into the woods. His knees are shaky and his footsteps uncertain, but without thinking, he tiptoes around his puke and joins the trail leading away from the house and follows its meander down the side of the hill a few hundred yards until he hears running water. Then, before him, a creek, casting itself over jags of stone, the slender light popping across its peaks, and immediately he is kneeling on its bank, gulping at palmfuls of water and rubbing it over his lips and cheeks and hair. He drinks like he's drowning himself. Slurps the water between his teeth to wash away the grit of vomit. Around him the forest whispers for him to go away, go away, go away quickly.

You'll catch me? Grace had said.

I'll catch you. Tim standing belly-deep in the pool of water that collected at the base of the flat stone. Their stone. Their water.

Above him, Grace, flat-footed and shivering, her arms drawn to her bare chest, her smile drawn crooked with cold. I'm coming, she said.

Come on, then.

Okay. Alright.

She backed up several paces and ran and launched herself from the stone and cleared his waiting arms and landed on the other side of him, tucked for an explosion. The pool shimmered in her wake and washed against the shoreline and he stood wiping water out of his eyes and when he opened them again, she was in front of him, her mouth wide and the beautiful air coming in and out. She jumped and wrapped her legs around his waist and tucked her face into his neck and he had the strange thought that it would have been a perfect moment to die.

Their first winter in the cut was nasty, and the following spring the creek swelled with snowmelt and slipped its banks and began inching its way toward the house. By noon of the first day it was halfway across the yard, by dinnertime licking the cornerposts of the porch. They stood in the doorway and looked out on their newfound river, the diving rock submerged and a cowlick of current swirling where it should have been. He waded out and hustled John up the hill to the barn where the sheep had been shrieking all day like children. The old man looked at him and ground his teeth. *Don't leave me here with these bastards*.

The water got high enough to dampen the floor of the porch and seep into the holes of the foundation. The worst of it avoided, but still they'd been warned: this is what Mother Nature could do should she feel the need, should they neglect to recognize her, should they not pay the proper respects. There were a thousand ways for her to stand up and bite them.

He wakes with his back to a stump and the forest alive around him. The creek wider than before, golden in the sunlight, whisking at the detritus of its haunches. At his feet, another place where he's lost his guts. He tries to stand, wobbles, steadies. When the wind is gentle, he can smell himself. There is soap in the trailer but he skips it, strips naked and wades carefully into the creek. The rocks slick with algae, he holds his hands to his sides like a circus performer and finds a spot deep enough to sit in. The shock of frigid water pulls him into himself, propels a gasp from the pit of him and shoots it through the trees. He sits with his mouth hanging open and his eyes cinched.

This, he decides. This is where. A place of quiet and anonymity; a place to sleep that reminds him how he misses the comfort of Grace's body, her warmth, her breathing. He will spend some time with her here, with her memory, give himself over to grief where no one can watch him or distract him or try to stop what his mind has already put in motion.

What if I come with you? Where you go, I go?

And then, there she is: the girl from the restaurant, from the photographs, climbing the creek downstream, head low and fingers grappling carefully at stones, jeans rolled to the knees, a muddy sweatshirt, sneakers tied together and draped around her neck. He can hear her breathing, talking to herself, and there is a moment of panic—that he's naked, that he's nowhere he's supposed to be, that it had to be this particular person at this particular moment who found him. But before he can make the decision to stand and run, she rises, no more than twenty feet between them, and stops. Looks at him this way and that, adjusting her head to catch his different angles.

Peaches, she says. You didn't make it far.

All of their feet rotted away, but Goodell got it the worst. Tim remembers him at the top of a hill overlooking a thousand acres of rice paddy, his one leg crossed over the other and his chin jutted forward as he used his fingernail to peel off bandage-sized strips of skin. The bottoms of his feet like cracked hams, his face the color of boiled meat. For all his nocturnal searching, his crazed intention to become a native species of the Asian wilderness, Dean Goodell was still very much human, and thereby subject to the laws of human affliction. He withheld his regard for the hand Nature had dealt him and she, in turn, withheld her own regard for him.

They offered him spare socks, laces to replace the ones on his boots that had frayed and snapped and been reinforced with twist-ties and cotter pins.

Goddammit, corporal, take care of your fucking boots, Lieutenant Sizemore said. I won't let you leave here because you're too fucking dumb to tie your shoes. And Goodell sat cradling his foot like a sandwich and looked up at the lieutenant and smiled.

He didn't, of course, take anyone's advice. Instead he strapped his boots to his pack and went barefoot for two weeks until Sizemore had no choice but to send him for treatment. While he was gone they talked about how nice it was to not have to hear his voice, to not have to smell fish on his breath when he barked out laughing, but then one morning they woke to find him squatting in the center of their bivouac, stuffing pieces of Juicy Fruit into his cheek and waving at each of them: Hello, good morning, welcome to Vietnam.

Tim sometimes considered killing Dean Goodell. They all did.

Don't do nothing stupid, Lieutenant Sizemore told them one night while Goodell was still away. If you kill him, he'll come back as a bat, and you'll wake up with Dean Goodell slurping blood out of your fucking pecker.

All summer they went to the water. Lay beside it, read paperbacks with their toes in the creekbank mud. They ate dinner on the diving rock, bowls of spaghetti that scraped when they set them down; they began fidgeting with each other, shamelessly reaching between the buttons of each other's clothes. The water and the sound of the water, she said, were what made her love it there; that they could lie awake at night with the window open and hear a vein of the earth pumping its own blood, the health in cool water, the strong resemblance it drew to human vital signs.

I don't love it in the basement, he'd said, and Grace had looked at him with empty eyes.

Every living thing gets big for its britches, she said.

What about living things that don't wear britches?

Even them.

I'd be afraid to see some things in britches, he said. Wolves. I wouldn't want to see a wolf in britches.

You've seen plenty of wolves in britches, she said, and when she finally laughed, her stomach pistoned up and down and her tongue slid between her teeth.

The rock was for their best times and their worst times. They argued there nearly as often as they didn't. No matter what, they could always just leap off and sink and come up for air clean and huffing and forgetful.

The girl stands with little horseshoes of water circling her legs. She has a round stone in one hand and a forked stick in the other, maybe for protection. Tim dries his hair with his shirt and forces his wet legs into his jeans.

You aren't working today, he says.

She watches him as though they're old friends at a sleepover. Nope, she says. Day off.

He finds her ease with him strange, that she seems to have no qualms about watching him dress, that she has not yet questioned what he's doing here; she plants her stick into the creekbed and leans on it like an explorer. Her shoulders broad and strong. Her legs stout. She has a line of freckles across the bridge of her nose from one cheek to the other.

Did you get lost in the storm, she says.

He sits on the stump and stretches his wet shirt over his head. I guess I must have, he says.

Easy enough to do.

I'm living proof of it.

You found a place to camp?

I did, he says. Up the hill there.

So Jonas was right. You're a camper.

Well, he says, and looks upstream to where the creek disappears over the top of the hill. I don't really know what the right word for me is.

She kneels and snaps her hand into the water. A second later she brings it back up and shows him the belly of a struggling crawdaddy. She puts it back in and splashes to scare it away and looks at him again.

Widower, she says.

He's made his hands into suction cups against his ears, trying to drain water. What's that, he says.

That's the word for you, she says. Widower. That's right, ain't it?

He drops his hands to his lap. Well, don't you got me pegged.

Her eyes are large and gray, like hurricanes. I got everyone pegged, she says. It's a talent.

Well then, it's only fair. What's the right word for you?

Sadler, she says. My name is Sadler.

Plans

HIS WHOLE LIFE, Tim granted Anthony the better parts of living. The bigger bedroom, the easier chores. Once, they'd both had their eye on a beautiful tenth-grader named Heather Coffee; Tim was in the ninth grade, Anthony the eleventh. Tim, as usual, deferred to his brother, who scraped together enough money to take Heather to a Walter Mathau flick called *Fail Safe* and claimed they'd made out behind the theater for at least seven minutes.

What was it like, Tim had asked.

She actually kind of sucked at it, Anthony said.

Well, at least you got to see *Fail Safe*.

That's true, Anthony said. It was spot-on.

Mostly this system of deferment worked in Tim's favor. Anthony could be hard and intimidating. He had fists like cans of corn. He was not one to swing often, but when he swung, his opponent was disinclined to wait for him to do it again. The handful of fistfights Tim had seen him in had each ended in stammered apology from the other side, the beaten dog slinking beneath the car. Only once had anyone gotten the drop on Anthony, and while he was struggling under the weight of a fat boy's arm, Anthony had called out, *Grab him!*, and Tim took a shot to the eye in getting the kid wrapped up. Anthony looked at his brother and beat the fat kid until the muscles in the kid's face tore and his nose hung sideways off his face. Afterward, he held Tim's chin with his fingertips. You'll have a helluva shiner, he said. But you'll be alright.

Tim assumed Anthony would always hold a physical advantage over him and over everybody else: always the faster cross, always the more vicious jab, the willingness to bite when grappling. Tim let his brother defend him when the situation demanded; otherwise, he tried to speak only when he knew Anthony would agree.

And then, war. Anthony became a Ranger and spent most of his time south of Saigon, mucking through the Mekong Delta, actively picking fights;

Tim, an average grunt in an average platoon who did anything he could to avoid enemy contact. They came home and sat at their mother's table and it was immediately clear that neither respected his brother's feelings about Vietnam: Anthony was still a soldier of liberation, a *warrior* in the truest sense of the word, while Tim was only furious that he'd been sent, furious that he'd gone, furious that he'd been there so long, furious that when he'd come home, nobody'd shown him anything but pity. He regarded the whole thing as a colossal, unplanned waste of time, a tragic loss of life. And so, they argued: an hour, two. Spitting their passions across the tablecloth. Their mother with her head on her fists. Once it started, she had no way to stop it.

Afterward he thanked his mother for dinner and went to the yard and fished in his pocket for keys.

Hey, Tim, his brother said from behind him, and Tim turned to look directly into the dark hollow of a Colt 1911, the same model his father had given Tim before he died. Anthony's was newer, slicker, better taken care of.

His brother pulled the hammer back and tensed his hand. Don't you ever fuckin, he said, shaking.

Don't ever what? Tim said. His hands flat at his waist.

This is *my* country, Anthony said. I live here. I love it like I want to. Don't you *ever*.

And instead of being afraid, Tim understood something then: his brother's advantage had always been bullshit. Tough words, sharp eyes, maybe the busted teeth of a few soft losers to drive home the point. If Anthony had ever actually wanted something from Tim, he could've simply shot him in the head and taken it. He was a coward like that.

Three children. Grace always claimed it a perfect number. She'd hoped for two girls and a boy, so Tim could still get dirty and the girls could gang up if need be. Three would give help on the farm; three was a pack of defenders against the outside world. A family of five left one chair at the table for guests. The math, she claimed, was sound.

But what about the math of money, he'd said.

Grace believed money came and went with the circumstances, that if she needed it, it would be there, and if she didn't, it would seek other folks. It was a charming idea, but bullshit.

We have money coming, she'd said. I can feel it.

That's good, because I can't.

Here's what he *could* feel: seventeen dollars in cash in his billfold, two hundred and twelve in the bank.

Besides, Grace said, we've got a couple of years to screw our heads on straight.

She walks back with him toward the trailer, deciding now and then to veer from the path and swing uphill from tree to tree like a chimpanzee. Her movements both strong and graceful; she is a product of the woods and knows to use her surroundings to her advantage. Footstep to forest floor, palm to branch: the sinews between Sadler and the natural world are strung tightly as a bow. When she leaps, she covers twice as much ground as a normal human should.

You're from around here, then, he says, panting. His legs burning. It's been a while since he, too, was a woodsman.

Just over the way, yep. She has peeled a strip of bark from a tree and goes along chewing it. Been a while since I was on this side of things.

He stops for a second to catch his breath. I was here a long time ago, he says. Me and my brother.

She turns and looks back down at him. I know you were.

They talked to each other constantly, though it was a rare occasion that anyone said anything meaningful. Melrose and Popp and Gessner a tight group, always on the periphery; Burns and Ocasio and Maksik and Shepard the sports fanatics. Maksik kept a deflated soccer ball in his pack. They blew it up and played whenever the platoon came to a patch of grass. They all talked about women and movies and the Giants and the Bears and the Yankees.

No one talked to Goodell, and he seemed to like it that way.

Once, only one time, did Tim ever talk about anything real with Lieutenant Kenny Sizemore. A Saturday at the rear, a nice day. Sun, beers. Burns and Ocasio and Maksik and Shepard playing two-on-two on a riverbank. Sizemore leaned against a rock, watching, smiling, laughing when one of them fell in the sand or caught an elbow or called someone else a cocksucker. Tim hadn't noticed him and wandered over to see the game for himself.

Hey cocksucker, Sizemore had said. Down in front.

Sorry, Tim said. He moved back and sat beside the lieutenant.

So, how's your vacation, Sizemore said.

Dogshit, sir.

Sizemore grunted. Yeah, well. You could write your congressman.

My congressman is also dogshit, sir.

Maybe when you get home you can take his job.

That'll be the day.

Sizemore reached into a box by his hip and pulled out a Budweiser and handed it to Tim. Drink up, he said. Tomorrow it's back to paradise. He looked over. By the way, I never asked where you were from.

West Virginia, sir, Tim said.

Jesus fucking Christ, Sizemore said. Maybe this really *is* paradise for you, then.

Tim smiled. We have our good days and our bad days. What about you?

I'm from Port Arthur, Texas, Sizemore said. You wouldn't know it.

You're right. I wouldn't.

Sizemore stretched and groaned and closed his eyes. Leaned back against the rock. It's where I'll make my fortune. Just you watch.

That so, sir? What is it you're thinking?

I dunno, Sizemore said. Selling dope, probably.

A boy will be named Charles, and a girl Winifred, but we'll call her Winnie. The other girl will be Caroline. What do you think?

Charles sounds like a king's name.

And for good reason.

Why name someone Winifred if you want to call her Winnie? Why not just name her Winnie?

Why name someone Timothy when you want to call him Tim?

Okay, well. But Anthony was never Tony.

Which is good. He doesn't look like a Tony.

Nope. He looks like a dickhead.

Well. Your parents could hardly have gotten away with naming their child Dickhead.

You'd like to think, but for him, people might have understood.

Sadler stands in the trailer's yard as though frozen to the ground. Her arms by her sides. The rippled teeth of creekwater still nicking the cuffs of her blue jeans. A sheen of sweat at her temples. She regards the house carefully: its busted windows and drooping corners. Muddied in a long-ago rainstorm. Patches of brown puke warm and obvious in the sunlight.

I'll be damned, she says. Here it is.

This place means something to you, he says.

Sure it does. This is my grandparents' house.

He tries to gauge her take on this, on him, on finding a place she seems to have lost. Staying the night had seemed, at first, like a necessity of survival. Then, a convenience to keep from pitching a tent. Now, though, any plan to stay longer strikes him as an invasion of privacy. An intrusion.

She starts toward the stoop with broad, meaningful strides. Says, I can't believe you slept in this shithole.

That night he lay in his tent listening to river wake lap against the shore. Voices from somewhere. The soft pump of rock and roll through a shitty transistor. Quiet nights impossible to sleep through. Without the roar, the percussion, the incredible monotonous neck-breathing of the Vietnam wind, they were without their lullaby and hopeless because of it. He knew for certain each man in the platoon was awake. To fall asleep in silence was to drown.

As if in confirmation, someone rapped his wooden tent stake and whispered, Country, Country.

Come in, Tim said.

Dean Goodell twisted himself into the tent and sat in the dirt beside Tim's feet. Country, he said.

Can't sleep?

Same, Goodell whispered.

It was a question.

Oh. Fuck me.

Tim with his eyes cinched, though Goodell wouldn't have seen that. What is it, Goodell?

Goodell sighed. I come to bid you farewell.

The fuck is that supposed to mean?

He could hear Goodell's lips crack when he smiled.

I'm leaving tonight, Goodell said. My training is complete.

Your training?

I've become a ghost, Goodell said.

Tim opened his eyes and turned toward Goodell, could only see the black outline of the soldier's body, like a gorilla calmly waiting for something to move.

You're full of shit, he said.

Me ask you a question, Goodell said. You heard me talking to anyone at night? Think back. Two, three weeks. Anyone say my name?

Nobody likes you, Goodell. No one says anything to you or about you.

No, Country. Jesus, you're an asshole. The reason nobody talks to me at night is because I'm not here. I haven't slept within two miles of this platoon in almost a month.

Tim knew from the sound of Goodell's voice that he was telling the truth.

So where you headed?

Bac Lieu. There's a road I can follow from there to Kuala Lumpur. After that, maybe Bali.

Bali?

Fuckin A right, Bali.

What about home?

Goodell laughed. Home? Fuck home. Home sent me here.

* * *

He stands at the kitchen counter, fingers laced at his belt, watching her explore. She moves in and out of spaces quickly. Peeks into the closet long enough to smell its air, closes it. The bathroom and its plant life, sprouting between tub and linoleum: small tan mushrooms, stray weeds. The cracked bar of soap still on the shelf. When she's finished, she comes back to the living room and stands beside his mattress.

Nothing much changed, she says, and waits a beat before smiling.

Listen, he says. I'm just on my way out.

No, no, stay. Nobody lives here. It ain't doing no good for anybody else. You go on and do what you got to do.

He turns to the wall with the buckshot holes. How is it you think you know so much about me?

She shrugs, kicks one of the empty beer cans on the carpet. Says, It's a gift.

No, really.

Alright, then, Peaches, she says, ignoring him, clapping dust from her hands. I'll leave you to it. She steps over the mattress and hops onto the stoop, starts across the yard toward the driveway.

He leans against the door and watches her go. Hey, he says, and she turns.

Leave it alone, Peaches, she says. I just know things. Only God knows why, but being right ain't something worth questioning. Being wrong is. You tell me I'm wrong, you can ask me more questions.

Animal

HE LEANS OVER THE OPEN DUFFEL and twists his mouth. He'd been so hurried to get out of the cut he'd neglected to pack anything useful: canned food, coffee. The initial plan to find someplace quiet, a nice felled tree to lean against, to watch the sky change until the moment seemed right to load his brain with a charge from the 1911. Sunset. Thunderstorm. Wait for the signal. When she gives you the signal, go and find her.

He's decided this place will do, but it doesn't yet seem time, and he's hungry.

He strips the lace from a boot and notches it onto a stick, snaps the ring from a beer can and bends it over and over until it breaks on one side, bends the sharp edge away to make a hook. Pulls out the book he packed—*Slaughterhouse Five*, something Grace had started and never finished—and walks back down the hillside to the creek.

He's opened his eyes to this water now three separate times, and each time it's been different: its path desperate or loping, its voice drawn together like a chord or, as now, burbling in a thousand tongues. He wanders downstream a ways to a spot where it draws together into a pool. Gets on his hands and knees and begins flipping rocks, searching for crawdads. When he finds one, he snaps it into pieces and slides part of its body over the makeshift hook. Polishes it to a sheen with its own guts. Then he sits back on the creekbank and drops the line into the pool and waits.

One night, early fall, a pair of coyotes came by the house. Tim watched while they parted the trees on the water's near shore, the setting sun their cover, slinking shadow to shadow. They spent several minutes drinking, but when the sheep began to bray, they cocked their heads toward the barn and sniffed the air with their eyes closed. Tim on the back of the couch, looking out the window, 12-gauge across his knees. Their fur the pink and orange of the sky so that when they trotted, it seemed they had backs of flame.

Grace watched him watching them. No secret that his willingness to protect was absolute. She chewed a fingernail and smiled, knowing he would shoot the dogs to keep them away from the sheep, from Old Man John. It wasn't that she enjoyed death, she'd once told him; it was that she enjoyed having someone near who could bring it should the situation arise.

Tim slipped from the couch and into the kitchen, watched the coyotes crossing into the side yard, followed them to the rear, eased the screen door open, stepped into the grass. His feet bare in the cool evening damp. The coyotes paused when he swung the shotgun to his shoulder. Twenty feet away, maybe. Fifteen. Their bravery a kind of ignorance. He pulled the trigger and blasted the lead dog into the weeds. The second one, a female, looked at him for a split second, her eyes wide like a human's, and bolted.

They'd gotten used to Goodell looking shabby and restless at roll, but when he didn't show up at all the next morning, it jarred them. The whole time thinking he was crazy, delusional, a little full of shit. And now.

My training is complete, Tim thought, and smiled, and said Gone, sir, when Sizemore called Goodell's name.

He's sixty-six pages into *Slaughterhouse Five* before he gets the first interest in his bait. The stick stuffed into his boot to keep his hands free. It wiggles, jerks, and he lays the book down beside him and pulls the shoelace out. A thick, shiny rainbow trout dangling from the makeshift hook. Angrily flailing for its life. He goes to grab it but it slips from his fingers, swings skyward, tears free, tumbles back into the water. The crawdad bait stolen, a bit of flesh ripped from the rainbow's cheek and stuck there in its place.

Motherfucker, Tim says. He leans over the pool but the fish is long gone.

He loads the hook again with a sliver of crawdad torso. Casts the lace into the pool, picks the book up.

The female came back again and again. Twice, three times a week, out of the woods, down through the field to the creekbank, where she would stand and drink and look up at the house. Never as close as she'd gotten before with her mate, but close enough that they knew she was there, that they could catch her woody mildew scent on a breeze. They knew they might wake one morning to find their barn an abattoir. He'd patched its holes and corners with fresh wood, looped a thick chain through the door handles; still, there was never any telling where anger could go, what small spaces it was capable of sliding into.

Why return to devastation? That evening in these woods, years ago, with his brother: it had been the last one. They had never done it again. In short order they would both be in the jungle, shooting at ghosts, forgetting the other's face, the sound of his snoring, the print of his boot as they walked single-file through the brush. A way of life had ended, and though he's never considered it before now, Tim knows it was his fault.

He jostles the line limply and stares out across the water, half-expecting to see Anthony on the opposite side, doing the same thing, reading the same book, casting for the same fish. When they were young, they'd looked alike but grew away from each other with age: Tim's face had rounded, his beard grown in patchy, his eyes darkened nearly to black, while Anthony stretched long and thin, rawboned like a rodeo, wiry as their father. Anthony strongly resembled the paternal side of the family, a fact which caused him both pride and shame in alternate measure. He was unpopular with girls, unpopular with teachers, unpopular period. Viewed it as everyone else's fault rather than his. He took to camping often while Tim desperately chased junior-high tail; Anthony teaching himself to field dress rabbit while Tim learned to unhook a bra single-handed. It took Tim some years, and no small measure of rejection, to finally join his older brother in the woods.

What if someone had told them they might need each other one day, a white lie to keep them together? Anthony was almost thirty and still living in the rental house with their mama. He had long suffered dreams of war. Would they have become a team again, ever? What if their mama had convinced Tim to stay that night, that dinner when Anthony pulled the gun? Would they eventually have killed each other?

He catches a snag on the line and pulls it gently. Another bite. He jerks upward to sink the metal barb in, then upward again, and another rainbow—smaller, darker—flips out of the water, wrestles with the world for its life. This one he manages to catch in his fist and unhook. *Mam-ma, mam-ma*, it says, and with a quick tense of its muscles it slips from between his fingers and plops back into the current.

Motherfucker, he yells. Goddammit, you motherfucker, and he thrusts his bare hands into the creek and grabs at nothing. The fish long gone again. Goddammit, you motherfucker, he says. His shins dig into the rocks. He sinks his fingers into the creekbed and squeezes. Cocksucking motherfucker, he says. His voice bounces off the trees and comes back like a dropped bundle of sticks.

And then, for a minute, silence. His wet hands on his knees. His chest heaving. Around him the forest, too, breathes deeply.

❧ ❧ ❧

On the far side of camp Gessner found a tunnel through the brush where Goodell must have passed on. Like a bear's den, a hole to nowhere.

Sizemore clearly considered it a problem. I don't want anybody getting any ideas, he said. We're liable to find him rotting like an old fish sooner or later. As though they'd had any inclination to do the same thing. As though any of them had the gumption to walk all the way to fucking Bali. For emphasis, Sizemore conjured an image of Dean Goodell's corpse: stripped and flayed open and his organs spilled out into the leaves. In Sizemore's version of Goodell's future, wild pigs crunched at his balls and snakes slithered out of his asshole.

An undeniable truth was that Vietnam was a worse place without Goodell. They hated him, but their hatred had been of an innocent brand: the same they felt for their sisters, whom they also loved, or that they'd felt for vegetables when they'd been boys, helpless and defeated at their mothers' tables. More annoyance than nemesis. Now that Goodell was gone they'd have to focus their hate on more tangible things: the heat, the leeches, the breakup letters they got in the mail, the motherfucking Vietnamese.

Sometimes she would stand out in the woods and call. Short barks followed by a disgraceful keening. At night they lay in bed listening to her.

I did her a disservice, not killing her, he said.

I doubt she sees it that way, Grace said.

I don't doubt for a minute she sees it that way. Jesus, listen to that.

Is that sadness? Grace said. Tugging gently at the waistband of his briefs. I'm not sure that sounds like sadness.

Could be sadness, could be anger, could be both. Anyway, they all sound the same.

Let's make a different sound, she said. Maybe she'll go drown her sorrows elsewhere.

He said, I just can't get over that wailing. Jesus.

The sun nearly at full noon and his pool gone dry of fish. A couple more have come and gone in brief visits of pity, none of them hungry to partake, but now his line dangles in an empty bucket. His stomach drawn tight. He tries to ignore it with *Slaughterhouse Five*, glances around now and then in mock contemplation, but if he aims to live long enough to serve his honor, to wait for Grace to come back and tell him the path is clear, he'll need to eat something. Amazing how even in the most extraordinary of circumstances life's daily chores just keep needing done.

He needs fresh bait, so he flips a river stone and looks underneath: nothing. He flips another and a fat crawdaddy scampers sideways. He flicks his hand out and snatches it by the tail, just as the girl Sadler had done, lifts it out of the water to look at it up close. The black eyes, the slow pincers. Then, in a fit, he snaps its arms off where they meet the body and drops them. He bites the animal in half and chews. It is disgusting in no way he's ever known before. Warm guts between his teeth. The snap of the eyeballs. Bitter in the brains but slightly sweet of the flesh. It takes great strength to swallow. He thinks solemnly of Goodell, of the fish guts on his chin. Then he pops the other half in, chews at the grit that coats the shell, the wiry hairs of the swimmerets, the tough sticks for legs, and swallows again.

Clarity

THAT EVENING HE LIES ON THE MATTRESS in the grip of a terrible cramping. He has retched for an hour, vomited once, nearly shat himself on four occasions before running outside and crouching in the weeds. His shirt bunched and clamped between his teeth. Tugging at the denim of his jeans to keep himself from trying to rip his own stomach open. His eyes sore from the bulging pressure of convulsion, his throat burning from the hacking, the shredded noises he makes when he gags. Outside, his second night on the hillside is coming on: cicadas and bullfrogs, crickets, the myriad footsteps of any number of predators.

Between moments of intense pain, though, a surprise: tender seconds of clarity, minor atmospheric changes of the type that make a second person noticeable in a pitch-black room. The walls of the trailer expanding and contracting like lungs. There is time to think, within one of these blessed pauses, of what Grace must have meant when she'd questioned his plans to come with her when she died: *What the fuck are you talking about*, she'd said, but what she'd meant was, *What do you know about suicide?* What she'd meant was, *What do you know about anything being final?*

How much he knew, though, that he'd never felt it right to tell her. How much he knew about the deceptive heartbreak of finality.

Three weeks after Goodell went AWOL, Ocasio used two belts to hang himself from a defoliated hopea tree. He'd done it at night: waited until his watch, walked a few yards from his tent, killed himself silently. No fuss for his friends. No conversation. They'd found him at daybreak with his pants half torn off, some animal sensing easy meat but chased away by a sleeping man's fart or a coughing fit in the night.

In the real world, it would be a thing that needed made sense of. A life cut short. A desperate action. In the real world the eulogy would have been a pleading interrogation of God's motives. Mourners would have worn black, a loose circle around the grave, a tumbler of scotch, a handful of peanuts from someone's grandmother's serving dish in someone else's family room. The shock of it wearing everyone thin.

But here, Tim thought, Ocasio's choice was totally understandable. No sense needed be made; it was already the most sensible thing. They stood around that morning thanking God for taking their friend, for giving him the strength to do what they themselves could only have hoped to do. Smoking in white t-shirts, boots loose, their hair unwashed. They helped load Ocasio's body onto a chopper and muttered how jealous they were that he was going home.

Around the same time, they got a letter from Dean Goodell.

He wakes to screaming in the trees. His heart pounding and a deep soreness in his belly, the tongue-taste of old pennies. Outside: the sounds of someone being murdered, a baby cast from a cliff. The noise fills the darkness and he swallows it and it vibrates though his chest and guts. He takes the 1911 from under the balled shirt he's used as a pillow and steps onto the porch. Cocks it and aims into the nighttime, into the gaps between the trees, but the world is empty. Gray clouds resting across limbs like playful lovers. He feels a twist in his intestine and sits carefully on the stairs. The moon behind a cloud, the lack of light incredible.

Then the sound again. A terrific, piercing shriek, like a woman burned alive or cut open belly to throat. He casts the gun uselessly in front of him. There is nothing to shoot at.

For some reason, though his nerves are frayed and his body shivering, he thinks of a night when he'd awakened in surprise and tried to touch Grace but came up with nothing, a handful of sheet, and heard her moving in the kitchen, seen the shadow of her slipping down the hallway, smelled the wake she'd left when she stood. She'd been making herself tea, an unusual late-night craving, and sat in bed for an hour sipping it with the light off and Tim beside her the whole time pretending to be asleep, pretending she'd never disturbed him. He thought it a kindness: she'd never know he'd been with her, nervous and confused, that he'd thought for a minute she'd died while he wasn't looking, that he was afraid he might have slept through it, and through her funeral, and through some unknown portion of whatever life it was that came after.

Then, in the quiet, a shift on a high branch, a sliver of moonlight, and he sees her: a screech owl the size of a small child, eying him with fleeting interest. Now and then she turns away and back again as if to make sure he's still there. He can't tell if she wants him to leave or is hopeful that he'll stay. He can't understand what it is she's trying to tell him. Her eyes are big and yellow—glowing, almost, pleading—and each time she snaps them shut, a millisecond at most, the world goes completely dark.

Boys, the letter began, and they hooted and laughed and cursed when Sizemore read it, the balls on this motherfucker, calling them *boys* as though he were somehow grander than them, as though they'd liked him more than they had. *Boys,* Sizemore began again, *I'm sorry to say that life is much better NOT in Vietnam.*

Tear that shit up, Maksik had yelled.

I'm drinking terrible coffee beneath a Coca-Cola sign in Bangkok, Sizemore read, *and here are the things I've learned: Thai food sucks. Thai beer sucks. Thai whores suck like fourteen-year-olds. Ha!*

My sister is fourteen, someone in the group said. This motherfucker's twisted.

When I was fourteen I could only get head from my pillow, someone else said.

I hope one of them whores cuts off his prick and chokes him with it, Maksik said.

If you cocksuckers are gonna chat it up every time I read the next thing, Sizemore said, I'm done with this shit.

Naw, naw, they said. Go on, go on, go on.

This morning I saw a pack of GIs on R&R, Sizemore read. *One of them with no pants on. Walking around in his tighty whiteys, and everybody in his group busting his balls, and Maksik, I had a crystal-clear memory of you and Ocasio, when you were hammered and pretending to—*

Stop reading, Maksik said.

Come on, Maksik, someone protested. He doesn't fucking know. They meant about Ocasio, how just a couple days ago he'd been swinging from a limb.

Stop reading, Maksik said again, and Sizemore folded the letter up and put it in his shirt pocket.

Sometime between spring and summer, the female left. There was an instant understanding that a constant had ceased to be, as when someone stills a tapping foot, or when, in a moment of cosmic coincidence, everyone in a restaurant stops talking at once. A sound was there and then was not there.

Tim felt terrifically chastened because, in truth, her silence was far worse than her pining. When she was around, they'd known she was around and could at least gauge her distance with some kind of accuracy. Now, though, they came and went in compromise, opened the barn door with resignation, kept a close eye on where the dogs were and when. They let John graze in the yard though his withers were exposed and he was too old to fend for himself, and Tim would sit on the porch, eating fruit, reading, shotgun close at hand while the old horse got his fill. Their lives dictated by the absence more than they had ever been by the threat. Grace had been particularly maddened by the quiet.

Then, a hot summer day, she returned from a trip into Victory and got out of the Ford crying. Tim with the lawn mower, shirt tied around the handle, his skin pink. He cut the mower's engine.

Alright, he said. Alright. He wrapped her in his arms.

I just hit her with the truck, she said.

Hit who? Who'd you hit?

The coyote, she said. She pronounced it *kai-yote*. I think she's dead.

Our coyote?

She nodded. Tears in the corners of her lips.

Thank God, he said, and his relief was real.

They got into the truck and drove out the path a ways. Grace craning over the dash. Pointing, withdrawing, pointing, withdrawing.

There, she said, finally, and indeed there was a clump of dead beast in the ditch. Still, but for the fur of its haunch casting in the breeze.

He got out and stood over the bloodied animal for a minute, shotgun at his hip. Then he got back in.

It's not her, he said.

What?

It's not her. Just some old farm dog.

Bullshit.

He's wearing a collar, love.

Later in the afternoon he went back, alone, gathered up the dog in a blanket and took it down and buried it at the edge of the woods.

That night, Grace was restless in bed, turning and breathing, turning and breathing, before he asked her what she was thinking about.

I've told my brain to believe that that was our coyote, she said. And my brain will do what it's told.

Okay, he said.

I need that to have been our dog.

Okay. I understand.

She turned to him and propped her head on her fist. Do you believe it was her?

No, he said. I told you. It was just an old farm hound.

She huffed. How am I supposed to believe one thing while you believe something entirely opposite?

We could just let it be what it is, he said. Or else we could keep talking about it.

She is standing at the foot of his mattress when he wakes. The sun filling the trailer. A sharp, awful smell in the air like rotting poultry. His eyes take a minute adjusting, but when he can see her clearly, he knows she's smiling. Her hands on her hips. A gym teacher, a mother waiting for her boy to put on his shoes.

Mornin, Peaches, she says, and makes a show of looking around the room. Let's hope for a better today than what must have done yesterday.

He pulls himself into a sit and rubs the crown of his head. Wouldn't be hard, he says.

No, I don't expect it would be.

He sits there stupid for a minute. Sadler goes to the door and swings it open and the day spills in like a child at a party, happy but cautious, as though aware of some danger to itself.

I didn't know I'd be gaining any company, he says, sort of to himself.

She is wrestling with the sash of a window in the kitchen. That what I am? She grunts. Company?

I didn't mean it meanly, he says, stretching his arms into his t-shirt.

Of course you didn't. The sash flings open with a thump that shakes the house. Let a little Jesus in here, she says.

What he's seen when he's alone here and what he sees with the girl around are two different visions. The lonely vision one of depression, sadness, a spiral. The Sadler vision an overwhelming desire to clean up, to wash, to brush his teeth.

Come on, she says. I wasn't kidding. Let this place air out a little bit while we're gone.

Where are we going?

She glances at her children's wristwatch. It's almost time for church.

There is no bone in his body that wants to go to church, but his hesitation is short. *This could be it*, he thinks. *This could be the signal.*

Praise

HER MOTHER INSISTED THEY MARRY IN A CHURCH, though Tim had never been inside one and Grace had stopped attending when she got to college. She'd lied about it for years. Yes, of course I've met the preacher, she'd be saying on her dorm-room telephone. Tim silent on her bed. His name is Thompson, Erik Thompson, right, only he spells it with a K, like a Swede or something. And eventually her mother, appeased, would allow her to turn the conversation: to her grades, her roommate, which professors seemed worth their salt. Tim loved the game of tugging at pieces of her when she was on the phone, unbuttoning her corduroy pants, working as a team to silently lift her shirt over her head.

Statistics seems okay so far, she said, inching closer to him and to the bed. Everyone says it's the hardest, but maybe I'm just getting it. She turned away from him, phone cord around her waist, and let him put his hand down the front of her underwear. Nobody yet, she said, nobody serious, anyway, and she turned her head to wink at him while he pressed his fingers into her. That's not what I'm here for, anyway, she said, but her eyes were closed and she was biting her lip, barely paying attention.

She says she's proud of me for being so focused, she said, hanging up.

Of course, he said. Yeah, of course. Pulling his jeans to his knees. We're all so very proud of you. Eyes on the prize and all.

⁂

When they step out together he has no idea what time it is. Cool like morning, but bright. He thinks, not for the first time, that day and night in the forest may not be so different from heaven and hell.

Sadler has a blue backpack on and she's talking, but he only catches every fourth or fifth word. His stomach not okay. His head a wrung-out towel.

They walk past his busted truck and she eyes it cheerfully. Your trusty steed, she says.

He offers a chuckle. Not so trusty, he says.

Oh, give her some credit. She managed to land you here.

What makes you think it's a girl?

She stops and takes the truck in for a minute. Well just *look* at her, she says. And then: You know, there are people around who can fix you up.

I think I'm as fixed up as I'm gonna need to be, he says.

You're a strange ranger, Peaches.

If I'm not in the way, I mean. I'll do as I've been doing.

She looks up at him, keeps walking. You're not in the way.

At the dirt road they turn right and head up the hill another quarter mile or so. Soon enough, cars parked parallel in a line against the woods. Beat-down cars. Real-folk cars. Cars that probably have engines from other cars, pilfered when the other cars died their shitbox deaths.

Then, a clearing: a great green yard as though the mountain has cultivated a bald spot, a ring of evergreens around it like a stockade fence. He knows it immediately as the knoll from the pictures, and indeed the scene is the same: children run barefoot, close and churning and then far away and small as ants; women in house dresses, their underarm skin puckered and wobbly as they wave to each other in greeting. The man in the glasses is there, talking to a loose group of gentlemen in brown polyester slacks, their hair greased like teenagers. They keep the same jangly stance, backs hunched from years of God knows what kind of work.

The preacher's my daddy, Sadler says. They are in the thick of it now; several women have greeted them, children have run to the backs of Sadler's legs and gripped at her like she's a jungle gym. She shakes each of them off—women and children both—with a practiced smile, a laugh, a warmth that strikes Tim somehow as imitation. It isn't the same smile he'd seen when his eyes opened just a short while ago.

Which one's the preacher?

That one there, in the glasses, she says.

One day, not far from the coast, their platoon came across the still-smoking embers of what had been a small community temple. Its footprint scorched into the forest floor. Scalloped bits of paper streamer caught in the branches. There were times when they found scorched bodies, but this was not one of those times. It could have been the place was empty at the time. Could have been the remains had been dragged away by jungle dogs. The men poked around the wreckage sideways, with their other eyes and their weapons drawn to the forest, wary always of ambush. At back of the ruins sat a neat stack of cinder block, charred on the outside, but on the inside, an intact shrine: photographs in melted plastic sleeves, a pile of half-rotted bananas, metal trinkets, a pair of identical brass bowls. All of it mostly spared. Maksik reached in and took a banana, dropped the blacker half on the ground and stuffed the rest into his cheek. It's warm, he said, a bizarre grin on his face, and laughed through the meat. Then Lieutenant Sizemore, normally hobbled by his respect for the peasant way of life, whipped out his prick and pissed all over the block altar. Tim stood around with the other boys, laughing alongside them, watching Sizemore try to draw his name in the dirt before his piss ran dry.

Calvary Church of Jesus with Signs Following is warm inside and damp, like a terrarium or a locker room. Wood paneling over the walls and a wobbly ceiling fan low enough to make a tall man uncomfortable. Puke-colored linoleum on the floors. One open doorway seems to lead to a kitchen, another perhaps to a bathroom. He prefers not to consider the state of either.

Though the younger children have been left outside with the grandmothers, the number of bodies is still incredible. He estimates a hundred, a hundred and fifty, milling, chatting, touching their fingers to their breasts, shaking hands, telling each other how good it is to see you, how sorry I am, how helpful your brother was, how delicious that baked chicken. They seem mostly content, their faces of satisfaction, husbands proudly holding the elbows of wives, wives turned around in metal folding chairs, ribbing husbands about their goatees, their television habits.

This one here, I caught him watching *Days* the other morning, a woman says.

You're a bird, Danielle, her husband says, his cheeks gone pink.

They seem not unlike a family, a great extended family, their small talk and pleasantries and decent clothes and the smell of potluck on their breath.

Sadler helps him weave through, gripping the pads of his first two fingers with the rough pads of her own. He watches the one-two of their faces as they pass: delighted smiles meant for the girl, pinched confusion for him. He tries to project some kind of confidence, though in truth, he's no surer of what he's doing here than they are.

The ceremony was more beautiful than he would have imagined. A group of Grace's friends had gone earlier in the morning and decorated loosely, tastefully: candles placed here and there, lace on the sides of the pews, several arrangements of tight white flowers that drew the eye, intentionally or not, toward the crucifix. Christ and his sad face, cast toward the lectern as though he were trying to read the preacher's notes.

Their families commingled because his was so much smaller than hers. His mother. An aunt he barely ever saw and her boy, a cousin he barely even knew. His brother not bothering. Maksik had come from Arkansas, where he was desperately trying to contain himself in the surprising presence of a family of his own. He'd dropped into Texas to pick up Sizemore and they'd come the rest of the way together, made a road trip out of it. It was good to see them, but Maksik was missing three fingers on one hand from something other than war, and it was all Tim could do not to stare. He knew Maksik would have hated the pity. The two former soldiers, glassy-eyed and half-drunk, sat behind Grace's mother and sister; during the ceremony, Tim could see the women stifling their laughter while his friends made crude jokes in their ears.

Heavenly father, we are gathered here today to celebrate the marriage of

❦ ❦ ❦

Before the service begins, he thinks he sees Grace at the far side of the room. Sadler has dragged him along a side wall to the front of the sanctuary, and she stands chatting with a group of people who might be her age. Tim glances across then and sees what can only be the back of his wife's head, and suddenly no vantage is good enough. He can hear his own heart. She is moving, shifting, as if unable to decide whether to stay or to go, to sit or to stand, and he moves and shifts with her.

Excuse me, he says, and pushes past Sadler and her friends and crosses the aisle.

She is standing amongst other churchgoers, wearing a dress she'd never have worn before she died. It is far too old-fashioned. Now and then she throws her head back, laughing. The men around her in adoration. It was always Grace's way. When he's near enough, he touches her shoulder and she turns and it's her.

Hi, he says. He has stopped breathing.

Hi, she says back.

I thought I saw you.

I'm certain that you did.

The men around her are smiling, casting glances at each other, but they've stopped making any noise.

You look, he says, but can't finish.

What? *Whole?* She laughs her laugh. There is no doubt that it's her.

He can't think of anything else to do, so he moves to hug her, to hold her. She stops him with a raised hand to the chest, blinks, and her eyes are empty sockets.

Grace, Jesus, he says.

She puts a hand to her face and ratchets free a set of dentures. A line of thick spit trailing from her gums.

Then Sadler is there. Tim, she says. Let's go. Come here.

Grace, what happened to you, he says.

Tim. She pulls him by the back of his shirt. Said it and meant it. Let's go.

With a few feet of distance he can see it isn't Grace at all and never was. The woman is old and withered and the men around her are not as young as they'd seemed.

Who the fuck is that, he says.

Can you just get over here?

Who the fuck is that?

❦ ❦ ❦

That night the rain rattled their tents for a while before a thunderstorm overtook them completely. After each clap, Maksik would call into the night: Holy shit, that one was a doozy.

Holy shit, that one was a doozy.

Holy shit, that one was a doozy.

Laughter from here and there.

Holy shit, that one was a doozy.

A few chuckles.

Holy shit, that one was a doozy.

And then Sizemore: Maksik, shut the fuck up before I slit your fucking throat.

Silence for a minute, and another thunderclap.

And Maksik, whispering: Holy shit, that one was a doozy.

Sounds

THEY BURIED HER IN THE YARD of the same church they were married in. Many of the same people in attendance, some in the very same seats. Her sister with a baby boy, Nolan, who'd cried himself to sleep during the eulogy though he'd met Grace only once and would never remember her face. Or maybe that was why.

Calvary's house band is a scraggly bunch. The youngest, on electric guitar, is fourteen or fifteen. A ratty mustache across his lip and his shirt buttoned tight to the throat. An older man on drums who warms up as though he's never sat at a kit before. Jerking and hectic. There is a fiddler, and another boy on bass who could be the guitarist's brother. The singer is overweight and with bangles on her arms and great golden earrings scratching at her shoulderpads.

When they fire up their instruments and launch into the first song, Tim nearly ducks at the sound: a noise both piercing and guttural, like the explosion of a land mine and its shrieking aftermath smashed together, a roar and a scream at once and from the same mouth. The singer interrupts:

They are covered by the blood
They are covered by the blood
My sins are all covered by the blood.

On his right a gigantic man wearing a mustard-stained shirt and denim work pants that taper into the slender necks of his boots. Already with his eyes closed. He claps his great hands with such energy that the pops ricochet from the ceiling and bounce around the room.

My iniquities so vast
Have been blotted out at last
My sins are all covered by the blood.

And on his left, Sadler, alone. Her eyes, too, are closed, but she is not dancing. She seems instead to be dreaming, or else praying, her lips moving slightly, as though she's just tasted something particularly delicious.

He received his first R&R at the end of the hottest week they'd seen in the jungle. Boarded the plane to Bangkok, several dozen other grunts shouting above the engines about the wicked things they were going to do to the whores they were going to buy. Competing to see who could be the vilest, as though degradation were sport. Tim listening with his eyes closed, sweat dripping from his hair into his ears. Now and then the grunts said something that made him smile despite himself.

He rode into the city in a *tuk-tuk* whose windshield did nothing to block the simmering air. The driver dropped him in front of a fruit market and he waded inside, curious, through a sea of jiggling bodies, middle-aged men with wire-rimmed glasses pushing him out of the way, barking commands he couldn't fathom. Old ladies squeezing past him as though he weren't even there. In a way they were right. He backed out and turned onto the road.

He looked for the Coca-Cola sign Goodell had written about, but there were hundreds of Coca-Cola signs. Thousands. In a city of three million, a Coca-Cola sign for everyone.

After an hour of walking he saw four Americans he recognized from the plane. Standing on the street, smoking, puzzling over a map. He went over.

You boys find something to get into?

The one with the map looked up. Well, he said. We hear somewheres around here's where the nasty bitches are. He pointed at his map. Sweet bitches. Pointed. Ugly bitches. Pointed. Old bitches. Pointed. Young bitches. We done found the thick bitches, but every single one of em was a guy in bitches' clothes.

Tim looked at him, then down at the map. Looked back up, blinking.

The soldier folded the map and stuffed it under his belt. We're going on tour, he said, and his friends laughed. He had bucked teeth and an Adam's apple that rolled up and down when he talked. You wanna tag along?

❦ ❦ ❦

The sound remains in the room long after the song is over. A vibration in the walls, the excited limbs of unsettled people. Tim stands still, his eardrums berated, and watches as the man in the glasses ambles to the lectern. The parishioners sit gently, adjust themselves, their wallets, their watches, the bits of hair in the back that shook loose while they were dancing.

The preacher smiles. His mouth is broad and his teeth are bright and straight. His mustache trimmed clean. He says:

I was talking to God the other day, sitting in my car down here by Leonard's Sinclair, because I'd just finished my lunch, which I ate from my lap like a heathen, and I was talking to God and God was telling me the story of Job, which I had not exactly forgotten but was not exactly thinking of, neither.

That's right, a woman in the crowd says.

That's right, a man says.

And God told me about Job's complaint, the preacher says. About how Job went to God and called him unjust for allowing the good folk of the world to suffer for no apparent reason.

Tell us why, someone says.

The preacher's voice suddenly gets louder, more fiery, crackling: The Lord He believed in Job, you know that? And when Satan offered up temptation, did Job back down? All that hardship was to see if Job might lose his faith, because the Lord believed in him, because He loved him.

He loves us all!

Some of you know I've lost my wife, the preacher says, quietly.

God rest her, someone says.

She was the light, someone else says.

I lost my wife, and still I know that things will be okay, because what I love most of all about Job's story is that God proves His righteousness, He proves His blessed infallibility, when he tells Job the honest-to-goodness truth. He don't beat around the bush and tell him lies, He tells him, Job, now there are things you aren't never going to know, and things you don't never want to know. But you just have to know, I got this.

Someone yells, He got it!

He got it, Lord!

Hallelujah, the preacher says.

Hallelujah, Lord!

Hallelujah, the preacher says.

Hallelujah, Lord!

Amen, Brother Dennis!

The preacher says, Let's pray.

⁂

He sat on a wooden bench in the front room of the whorehouse, watching koi slither past each other in an overstuffed aquarium. The pumping of his new friends and their girls all around him; the building small, the walls thin. The soldiers shouting terrible things at the girls, and the girls replying from rote: "Yes, it's good!" or "I love this, baby man!" Their voices small and reedy.

The woman behind the shabby desk flashed him a sour look.

Nothing you want here?

There's nothing I want here, he said. No offense.

Then why you're here?

I'm just waiting on my friends.

Phuh, she said. You get new friends. She smiled and her teeth were crooked and brown. I sell you some.

Some other day, he said.

She squinted at him. There will not come another day for you. This a one-day-only offer.

Thanks, he said, holding his hands up. I'll pass.

❦ ❦ ❦

At the interment Grace's sister put baby Nolan in the grass and let him bobble back and forth across the gravesites. Ripping at patches of grass with his chubby baby hands. The wind blowing his soft blond hair across his forehead. The gathered mourners paying him varied amounts of attention: the older ladies clucking in disapproval while the younger ones tipped their heads toward him discreetly, nickering at him, smiling, waving with their fingertips.

The Vietnamese boy sat on a headstone, kicking his feet. He watched Tim heave the first shovelful of dirt onto Grace's coffin and slid down, walked barefoot past Nolan and over the cemetery road and disappeared.

❦ ❦ ❦

After the prayer, the service is conducted by committee: an older gentleman with a belly over his belt stands to tell them about Jesus' love; a teenager stands to tell them, in his excited way, about the first time he looked the devil in the eye. All the while the crowd bolstering with commentary: *Amen, brother; tell it, brother; Hallelujah, Jesus*. The preacher standing in the corner with his eyes closed behind his glasses, smiling, nodding approval. Tim watches him, fascinated. The preacher is in the throes of something, some reverie, and as Tim sits there with his guts in a knot and his head throbbing, he finds himself, despite his entire life, wanting some of it for himself.

The last member to speak is the old woman missing her eyes. She's helped to the lectern by a woman who might be her daughter and a man who might be her son. Her eye sockets pruny bumps, her nose turned down like a tree root. The microphone picking up the clacking of her dentures. There is nothing of Grace in her now; he can't understand how there ever had been. Before she speaks, she turns toward him and beams.

We have new blood in the house, she says. Can we give Tim our love, and can we share with him God's love?

The crowd rumbles its approval.

He needs some of God's love right now, she says. He's hurting.

The Lord will provide, someone says.

Amen, the old woman says. The Lord will provide.

Jesus is love, Tim, someone else calls.

Amen, the old woman says. Jesus is love. Amen. Well, how long's it been since y'all heard the story of Jacob and Rachel?

When the soldiers emerged from their fantasies, they were pit-stained and red. They hiked their too-big trousers, having lost weight in the jungle, flattened their hair with pocket combs. They walked past the madam and one of them laid a twenty on her desk. Down payment, he said, for the same one again next time.

New girls all the time, she said. You come try a little of all.

The soldier smiled. Maybe I just will.

They stumbled onto the sidewalk and stood squinting down the street, gleefully adjusting their crotches and pulling at the cigarettes wedged between their teeth.

The one with the map slapped Tim on the shoulder. You sure finished up quick, he said.

I didn't go in.

You what? The soldier looked around, flabbergasted, at his friends. You didn't go *in?*

Whores aren't really my thing, Tim said.

Whores aren't really your thing.

Not really.

What *is* your thing, man? He took a step back. Wait, man, wait. Don't say it. Don't tell us you're a homo.

Tim punched him. Crushed the boy's cigarette into his lips, sparks spraying into his mustache, split a seam down one side of his nose. He punched him again. The other boys standing around as if they couldn't see what was happening. The one with the map fell on his butt and shouted something that wasn't a word.

Then, finally, Tim caught the first blow to his temple. A second one dropped him to his knees. They kicked him in the ribs, in the face, in the back when he tried to roll into the street. The sound of it like far-off artillery. He closed his eyes and took it, and when he opened them again, the soldiers were gone.

Mama

THE SERVICE LASTS ABOUT AN HOUR, and afterward everyone goes back as they were: into the yard, leaving as they'd come, small talk and embraces, the children still barefoot, their grandmothers tired and fanning themselves at picnic tables. Tim comes down from the porch and squints until his eyes adjust. Sadler has slipped into the melee, and though he feels a strong urge to simply walk away, he also thinks, without reason, that he should say goodbye.

New boy, someone shouts, but it doesn't register that the voice is talking to him. Then a heavy clap on the shoulder, and he turns to see the big man that had stood beside him a minute before. Hey, new boy, the man says. Come introduce yourself, would you?

To who?

To Brother Dennis, the man says. He'd like to say hello. The man sticks his paw out for Tim to shake. My name's Wiley. Welcome to the mountaintop.

Wiley rumbles through the milling crowd like a linebacker and Tim follows in his wake. His air smells of woodsmoke and meat. The tips of his long hair damp with sweat, his thick flannel shirt stretched tight in the afternoon sun. He grunts as he walks, nods his head at people who say hello but doesn't say hello back. They turn the corner of the building and there is a group of people sitting at a table in the shade. The preacher is there, and the woman with no eyes. Sadler in the grass at their feet, laid back as though sunbathing. She doesn't look at Tim.

You found him, the preacher says, standing. He crosses the grass to shake Tim's hand. His grip is loose and cool. He wears a serious expression: mustache downturned, eyes bunched and trembling. Name's Dennis McIntire, he says.

Tim, Tim says.

What did you think of the service?

Tim looks at Sadler for help, but still she pays him no attention. It was quite…lively, he says.

There's a good word for it, McIntire says. He looks Tim up and down, as though taking his measure. Hey, I think you know my little girl there already, but let me introduce you to Mama McIntire.

Anthony and Tim spent summer days on the riverbank, throwing sticks and arguing and trying to drown each other. Their bond solidified by a love that closely resembled hatred. They swam and fished and grew dark brown, so brown that when they returned to school in the fall, their teachers would have trouble recognizing them. They put crawdaddies in a bucket and tried to make them fight, which they sometimes did. Bet punches on the winner. Charliehorsed each other as hard as possible regardless of the outcome, and even if there was no outcome at all.

One Saturday, their mama gone to work cleaning a neighbor's house, Anthony bumped a crystal vase from its table and watched it shatter across the kitchen floor. A wedding present from their grandmother, said to be a hundred years old, though for the life of them they couldn't imagine why someone would keep such a thing for so long. Anthony, desperate, had done the thing no service with a jar of brown paste, and the decision was made soon after to leave out, to let their mother see for herself the sticky mess of her history, to let the punishment simmer before they came back with their tails between their legs. Important to compose a remorseful face, to give one's voice a believable whimper.

When they did finally slink in, wet as rugs and smelling as bad, their mother took a wooden spoon and clobbered the backs of their hands with it until the skin puckered and turned purple.

Who was it, she'd said, her hair flying when she brought the spoon down.

Not me, Anthony said.

Not me, Tim said.

And she'd only raged harder then: the boys holding out their hands under their own power, knowing to take them away would lead to worse. Her next words unforgettable:

I don't—*whack*—give a whore's fart—*whack*—about the goddamned vase—*whack*—but don't you ever—*whack*—ever—*whack*—lie to your mother. *Whackwhackwhackwhackwhack*, a flurry of blows sharp and violent enough that the boys forgot the pain, so busy were their brains in deciphering the terrible look on their mama's face.

I enjoyed your sermon, Tim tells Mama McIntire. His hand tight in her own, her face cocked to him, looking through him with her imagination.

Oh, I thought you would, she says. I haven't dusted that old tale off for some years now. No, it's one of my favorites. Her smile is empty; he glances at the table, sees that she's dropped her dentures into a glass of water. She holds his hand for what seems an extraordinary time and uses it to pull him close. You seemed frightened earlier.

I've had some hardship, he says. Sometimes my mind does things. I'm not sleeping much.

Her laugh is strong and piercing. Don't I know it! And hoo, that old cabin can get mighty cold at night, cain't it? And lonely? I'll tell ya.

And then all four of them—Mama McIntire, Brother Dennis, Wiley, Sadler—are looking at him. He tries to shrink away, though there isn't much place to go.

You don't have to go anywhere, Sadler says quickly, and Brother Dennis glares at her.

That's right, he says finally. That trailer is a far sight better than a tent is my estimation. Just show what respect you can, is all we ask.

That's the only reason I'm out there to begin with, Tim says.

Ain't you sweet, Mama McIntire says. No it ain't.

While it was true that Grace wanted children, it was also true that she'd been in no hurry to get them. A great misfortune: youth wasted on the young, they'd been too busy romping under the sheets like teenagers to try in earnest for a baby. By the time her desire was recognizable, she was sick; by the time it was unbearable, she was nearly gone. There was a night near the end when they talked it through: Grace reclining on the couch, a silk scarf on her head, a turtleneck. She was always cold. Tim with her feet in his lap, staring at the leaves of an aloe plant that sat atop the television.

I hope you'll find someone who will give you kids, she'd said.

I won't. I won't try.

You didn't try to get me, she said, and yet here I am.

It's different.

How different? You didn't know I was there and then there I was.

He looked at her thin face, her chapped lips. There was some other hand in that, then, he said. Something else that had its say.

She smiled. You don't even believe in God.

I didn't say God. But I do know that when we found each other, there was no helping it. The world wanted it that way, same reason water flows downhill.

So we were like gravity?

I said it, so I must have meant it.

They sat together quietly for a minute. Tim nervously rubbing the heel of her foot.

But, she said. You're the last stop on the family line. What about your name?

Anthony will take care of it.

Anthony's never taken care of anything in his life.

Baby, please. That's my brother.

❧ ❧ ❧

Sadler walks beside him, quiet, her head cast to the road. There is no telling what she's thinking.

They were ten and eleven when their father died. He'd been cruel enough to wait until they were older and well able to remember details. So it was that for a lifetime Tim would know these things:

In the cemetery, squirrels fought in the trees. The sound of them scrabbling and their desperate chatter. They dropped acorns onto the casket, and he and his brother broke into a fit of laughter.

There had been a man in the kitchen of their house. His face long gone, but he was tall and spoke in a gravelly baritone; when Tim passed on his way to the bathroom, the man had his hands on their mother's shoulders as though he were about to shake her. Years later she'd tell him this had probably been his grandfather. His daddy's daddy.

A soldier presented their mother with a crisply folded flag. It was the first and last time Tim ever saw it.

Anthony had found the body. The old man with a towel around his waist, his hair wet as though he'd washed for the occasion. Crumpled into the space between the toilet and the bathtub, his arm bent awkwardly across his face, just settled down for a nap. The 1911 on the floor beside his feet. More blood than you'd think a person should have.

And their mother. They had not seen their mother shed a single tear. Not seen her break down. Not seen her drink too much, or speed away with new men. Not seen her sit on the sofa with a pillow clutched to her throat. They'd been forced to move, unable to pay the mortgage on the house their father had always wanted. When they pulled up to the new rental, a half a mile of driveway that led to a two-bedroom shoebox nestled back into the woods like a frightened animal, she'd shut the car off and turned to face them.

This will become the house you were raised in. Not that last place.

Yes, ma'am, they said.

You are to forget that last place. The carpet, the yard, the color of your bedroom walls.

Yes, ma'am.

I will raise you here my goddamned self, she said. And we'll be happy. Things will be tough now and then, but we'll be happy.

Yes, ma'am, they said, but they couldn't have known then how right she'd be: about the forgetting, about the happiness.

When they reach his broken truck, she pulls her backpack down and fishes out two paper sacks with greasy bottoms. She hands one over. Inside is a chicken quarter, a slab of cornbread, a piece of chocolate cake, a plastic barrel of juice. He sits on the bumper and lets the smell of the food punch him in the nose. Several days since he's eaten anything like it, and then only what nibbles he could stomach. Grace's mother trying to push a bowl of beef stew on him. Go on, she'd said, you need to eat. The dutch oven from a neighbor, one of several her parents had acquired after Grace. It had taken all he had to tuck into a piece of meat.

But this day is not that day, and he tears through the chicken like an animal at carrion, snapping its tendons with his filthy teeth and lapping at its fat with his dry tongue.

Thanks, he says, chewing. Jesus Christ, that's good.

He hardly notices that Sadler's left her food in the bag. When he finishes the chicken quarter, he throws the bone into the weeds and she hands him her own.

I have more at home, she says. You need to eat.

He looks at her. The second woman to tell him something in the space of a week that he'd never before heard in all his days.

What was that all about back there, he says. At the church.

Mama McIntire takes some getting used to. I should have warned you.

That trailer used to be hers?

No. It was my mama's mama's. She's been there plenty, though. Folks are tight up here.

I could have sworn she was somebody else when I saw her.

She bends down to zip her backpack, slings it onto her shoulders. She mighta been, she says. Never know. You walk into that church, all bets are off.

1911

THE THIRD NIGHT. He sits on the porch, smoking, belly full from the second sack of food. He's punched a hole in Sadler's juice barrel and sips it sparingly, wanting it to last. The 1911 on the step beside him, whispering:

What is all this, anyway?

He tries to remember his original plan: find a quiet place. Wait for the signal. One more goodbye. Bang. How long had he expected it would take? How lonely did he think he'd have to get? How could he possibly have forgotten the existence of other people in the world?

And this fucking girl. This girl with the guts to walk in when he was sleeping. As though they were old friends. As though they meant something to each other. He wonders if she'll be the one to find him.

I was here a long time ago. Me and my brother.

I know you were.

If he sees her again he will tell her to leave him be. That he won't be trouble much longer. He will make sure to tell her not to check on him. He knows what it is to see something you can never forget. He doesn't want that for her.

He looks at the sky and watches the light from an airliner blink through tree branches. And the stars, which are endless, the shine from their insides exploding, consuming themselves, nothing but old fires burning quietly out.

When Anthony aimed the gun at Tim's face, he could smell the use in its barrel. Powder. Anger. The seared flesh of a VC forehead. He could sense the use of it in Anthony's eyes, which wouldn't keep still; they shifted from side-to-side and never settled on Tim. If Anthony fucked up and pulled the trigger his eyes wouldn't be there to see it.

❦ ❦ ❦

He decided he would teach her how to shoot. This was just after he'd landed the painting gig, a regular thing, seven to four, five days a week. There would be times when she was home alone. Many times. He wanted to know she was safe, or could at least defend herself if she wasn't.

They walked up the hill behind the house and stopped at a level spot. He had a grocery bag of cans and beer bottles. They set them in awkward spots, different distances. Treelimbs, tufts of grass, fenceposts within range. He brought four magazines and a box of shells so he could teach her to reload.

So what do I shoot first, she said.

Nothing. You don't shoot anything until I say.

She pouted.

He held up the 1911 between them. Listen to me. These things are not toys. The first thing you do is learn to draw it. Then you learn to hold it. Then you learn to aim it. Then you learn to put it back where it was. Then, maybe, I'll let you shoot something.

She looked at the sun, made a show of yawning. How long is this gonna take?

He ignored her. Showed her how to load a magazine, how to rack it, how to bring a round into the chamber.

Set the safety on, he said. When you draw it, it comes up like this and your second hand meets it at waist-level. You bring it forward with your elbows bent until it's on a line with the center of your chest. As it's coming up, you're using your thumb to flip the safety off. The safety stays on until you're ready to kill somebody.

Do you really think I'll ever have to—

Pop. He shot a beer bottle from the fencepost. It shattered silently behind the rapport of the pistol. *Pop. Pop. Pop.* Three cans in rapid succession. He turned his body and raised his hands. *Pop. Pop.* Two more cans twisted from the tree and landed in the dust. Then he pulled his arms back into himself, brought the pistol down into the holster at his hip.

She watched it all like she was unsure it was really happening. Jesus Christ, she said.

Did you see, he said, how I re-engaged the safety on the way down?

❦ ❦ ❦

He hears her before he sees her.

It must be close to midnight. He hasn't moved except to piss from the side of the porch. The night has a chill to it, a chill he's been enjoying, the kind of breeze that shivers the unprepared bone.

She is whistling a tune he thinks he knows and shuffling her feet over the rocks on the long driveway. When he looks down into the hollow nighttime, he can see just the speck of her, a white flicker like a firefly, a headless ghost drifting through a tunnel, and gradually her parts become clear: bare arms and legs, sockless feet in old green tennis shoes, her face, the damp blond hair pushed behind her ears.

Top of the mornin to you, Peaches, she says.

Late for a walk, he says, and stubs his smoke out on the porchrail.

She looks at her toy watch, holds it out to him. Can't see it, she says. Pretty dark.

She stops at the foot of the stairs. Her white dress is thin. He thinks it holds some intention.

I thought perhaps you were thinking about me, she said. And I wanted to come straighten out any misconceptions.

❦ ❦ ❦

A lot of wondering went into what Anthony did that night. Tim gone home, back into Victory, to the tiny rented house on Allen Street. Grace still in college and her absence everywhere: in the air, in the floorboards. Especially at night. He was eating like shit. Drinking too much. Work kept him reasonably in shape, but he could still feel a blackness growing, formless and cumbersome, in his gut.

He expected Anthony had landed in a ditch somewhere, on a park bench, leaned haphazardly against an alley wall. In his imagination his brother *lived* outside, though it wasn't really the case: their mother had reluctantly taken him in, and he stayed more or less permanently on the couch in her basement. But it was true that he was a wanderer, a nighthawk, more comfortable in nature than in luxury, even if that nature was a shuffling jungle of street-level drunks, pissing on other men's shoes or on a sleeping enemy's face, the rambling expletives of veterans and lunatics, corn-fed savages for whom life had done no recent favors. Anthony was at ease among the well-heeled gone rotten. It made it simple to justify his own shitty self-esteem.

That night when Anthony pulled his 1911 on him, Tim could think only of one time: not long before their father died, he'd taken them out to learn to handle a gun. Already a few beers in, not yet noon. They walked a long path that hugged a creek. The air like hot breath and tiny flying bugs invading their sweaty crevices.

Hold your hands above your head, their father had said, tired of listening to his boys complain. His pistol bobbing in the holster at his hip. A sack of cans in his fist.

Why, Anthony had said.

They go to the highest point on your body.

Be real, Anthony said.

Don't you fuckin talk to me like that.

Anyway, it didn't work. Tim walked with his hand in the air and gnats chewing on his eyelids.

They stopped at a clearing by the pond and their father chucked a half dozen cans onto the surface. Tim, he said, you stand here. Anthony, here. When the boys were flanking him like he wanted, he said, Now watch. He drew the pistol slowly, clasped it with both hands, flicked the safety off on its way up. Pulled the hammer, aimed, fired. The bullet *thunked* into bare water, three feet from the nearest can. Fuck me, he said, and fired again. *Thunk.* He unloaded the magazine, *pop-pop-pop-pop-pop*, and his shots made a pattern in the pond, like fireworks.

His boys looking up at him. His pride their pride, and not much of it to go around.

It's been a minute, their dad said.

Take your time, Anthony said. You'll get it.

❦ ❦ ❦

It's time to spill the beans, Sadler says.

They are in the trailer's living room, leaning against the wall, the nighttime around them black and total. Through the walls they can hear crickets in the sticks, bullfrogs in puddles.

I don't know what you want from me, he says.

Where were you headed? When your steed broke down?

I wasn't headed to anywhere.

Bullshit.

I was looking for a place, but I don't know what place. He can feel her hip against his, the hard muscle of it.

She says, What kind of a place?

A quiet one.

Well you've stumbled across quite the one here, haven't you?

Debatable.

That an insult?

Yes.

In that case, I'm insulted.

I'm okay with that.

A second of quiet, and then: So okay, let's say this is the place. What are you gonna do next?

He shuts his eyes and leans his head back. I'm gonna wait for the signal, he says.

What signal?

The one my wife gives me.

How you gonna know it when it comes?

I'll know.

And what happens then?

The end.

❦ ❦ ❦

Tim took quickly to marksmanship, to handling a weapon. Their father unstrapped the holster and laced Tim's belt through it and cinched the belt back up tight so the gun wouldn't drag his britches down.

Now remember what I said, their father said. He was back a couple paces, a can of beer, a cigarette between his lips. Squinting. Draw one, hands up two, safety three, straight out four, aim five, fire six.

Tim did it in one quick move. Pulled the hammer, blasted a can and watched it flip across the surface of the pond like a caught fish. Adjusted, fired again, another hit. Anthony beside him blank-faced. When the magazine was spent, their father touched Tim's arm.

Let's give your brother a try, he said.

Anthony took the spot Tim had taken and held his palm on the butt of the pistol like a gunslinger. He gazed out on the lake, flipped gnats away from his brow with his free hand.

Any time you want, son, their father said.

Anthony pulled the weapon and extended his arm sideways and blasted off seven rounds without his other hand and without aiming.

Goddammit, boy, their father said. That ain't what I showed you. He handed him another magazine. Do it right or go away.

Tim watched his brother reload, set his feet correctly, draw and steady and aim and fire. His first shot missed. He took a step forward, fired, missed again.

You shoot like me, their father said.

Anthony glared at him, waded ankle-deep into the pond and fired at the nearest can. Three, four feet away. He missed. He walked out knee-deep and pressed the steel mouth of the 1911 against the side of the can and fired. It sunk for a second and popped back up, taking a little water, a small hole torn in its midsection.

Guess that's how it's done, he said, stumbling out of the water, his pants dripping and his sneakers muddy.

Their father tilted his head and finished his beer. Tossed the can into the pond. It's one way, he said.

They've been sitting a while, listening to nothing, saying nothing, their legs pressed together, the room around them cool. He realizes that at some point she's taken his hand in her own. Finally, she exhales loudly.

I don't get you, she says.

That's cause there's nothing to get.

There's gotta be something to get.

For what it's worth, he says, I don't get you much, either.

Maybe let's just figure each other out, then, she says.

How's that?

In one silent, invisible move, she swings her leg over his and settles gently into his lap. Face-to-face. Her hands around the back of his neck. He can smell the sulfur of well water in her hair, the toothpaste she used before she came out. All part of a plan.

Wait, he says. Wait, but she settles farther onto him and he can feel her warmth, the tight skin drawn beneath her dress.

She doesn't say anything, just listens to him with her mouth against his cheek.

This isn't quiet, he says.

He hears her laugh, feels her fingers unbuckling his belt. Well, Peaches, she says. I can stay quiet if you can stay quiet.

Tower

I have to go.

I have to go.

Shhh, I'll see you soon. I have to go.

❦ ❦ ❦

When he wakes, she is gone. The impression of her on the mattress, his arm out as though he'd been holding her. Crickets. Bullfrogs. Still nighttime, or else very early morning. He listens for a minute, expecting voices, footsteps, but there is nothing. Soon enough he's asleep again, the cold air drifting over him, lying on top of him like a bad dream.

❦ ❦ ❦

After Bangkok he had a month and a half left of his tour. The days passed as they'd always done: a few of them atrocious, but mostly just a boring hike in the trees. Gessner took a fleck of tree bark in the eye—some sniper potshotting from across a valley—and was sent home. Maksik got shot twice, flesh wounds on the thigh and forearm, but field-dressed them himself and didn't tell anybody. Later he showed Tim the small channel a bullet had made above his wrist. It looked like someone had scooped his flesh out with a melon baller.

When he was finally done, he spent a week in Hawaii, taking extra-long showers and walking the warm shoreline of Waikiki. He gathered a pocketful of shells and brought them home in a paper bag, intending to give them to a girl he'd known in high school, a girl he'd been in silent love with for four years. Grace, whom he'd marry soon, whom he'd buy a house with, who would bear him his first son.

These are for you.

❦ ❦ ❦

There is a note on the counter beside a package of Pop-Tarts. He tears the foil open with his teeth, stands eating while he reads:

Peaches, I only had the one pocket, or I'd have brought you something better. Sorry to leave, I'm breakfast shift at the restaurant. Did you know about the fire tower? Go back to the pike and take the fork you <u>*wouldn't*</u> *take to get to the church. Walk a mile and there's a trail on the right-hand side. Climb it. Maybe you'll see what you're looking for. Love, S.*

Love, S.

Love, S.

Love, S.

The night before had been a rapture. A rapture he hadn't wanted and hadn't sought, but maybe that was the way with raptures. Maybe if you seek the thing you can never know it returns the favor by never showing up at all.

❦ ❦ ❦

Grace had taken the car one week to visit her parents, so the next time Tim had dinner with his mother she came out to get him. She squeezed him around his waist in the doorway of his tiny rented house. Her hair was getting thinner. Her whole body was getting thinner. She seemed shorter than when he'd seen her several weeks before, at the first dinner home with Anthony, the dinner with the pistol in the front yard.

He asked if she'd been eating.

Oh, you know, she'd said. Not too much. I pick at things here and there.

Why aren't you eating?

I don't know, Timothy. Things just haven't been tasting very good.

She was still driving his father's old Chevelle. Winding roads, the whip-crack of deciduous leaves through his open window. Rocks on one side and the holler on the other. A twist of metal braiding the only thing between them and a hundred-foot drop into the creekbed below. His mother an expert on these roads, as though she'd used her own fingernail to scratch them through the mountains.

How's Anthony, he said.

She didn't answer at first, kept her eyes focused on the road. Finally: It's just so nice to have you both back.

But how is he?

Oh, Timmy. I don't know. He's in one piece, and that's all that matters to me.

He walks down to the creek and strips and washes himself with soap. Digs the water into the itchy scruff of his beard, cleans his ears, his dick, his armpits. Calf-deep in the cool green stream, he stands for a minute and lets the air dry him, lets anyone watching see him, though of course there is no one. He pulls his clothes over damp skin and brushes his teeth and swishes with creekwater and spits.

He straps on his boots and tucks the 1911 into his waistband and hikes back up the hill, past the trailer, down the long driveway and past his busted truck, out to Sand Lick Pike, where he takes the fork he wouldn't take to get to the church and walks a mile and finds a trail cut into the woods on the right-hand side.

Tim walked into the house and set his overnight bag by his feet. Anthony in the recliner watching television. His socks dangling from the ends of his toes. Sweatpants. An old white undershirt. Bowl of cereal perched on the tiny hump of his stomach. What piece of him their mother swore had made it out of the jungle was unclear.

Hey, brother, Tim said.

Anthony acted as though he hadn't heard him.

Tim said, Ant?

Nothing.

Timmy, their mom said, closing the door hurriedly, taking off her coat. Leave him be.

Why isn't he saying hello?

Because I don't fucking care that you're here, Anthony said.

That's nice, Anthony, their mother said.

If you don't want answers don't ask questions, Anthony said.

❧ ❧ ❧

She's right; the fire tower is worth seeing. It sits on the western crest of the hill, opposite where the church would be on the other side, its far wall perched on a break of limestone that looks out over the valley: fifty miles or more of hazy blue-green watershed until the view breaks against an immense ridge that may be the beginning of Kentucky. He climbs forty stairs and steps gently onto the platform, a rickety handrail the only thing between him and a hillside full of broken rock and bramble. Vipers slithering over shattered glass. The bones of other men come to lose themselves in the hills.

The door is crusted but not locked. He bumps it open with his hip and steps inside. The smell of dusty bedclothes, unfinished wood, prior occupants and their cigarettes. Not an unpleasant smell. There is a metal chair in the corner, a writing desk with its face carved up. Anna and Ben '58. Go Away. Ricky and Shawna, their names surrounded by a cartoon heart with an arrow through its meat. At the window he can see the entire valley, the full sun, great sections of treetops swaying in the wind, their fresh spring leaves caught in the current of some invisible ocean. He runs his fingers over the writing desk and steps back outside.

Spring in the mountains carries the weight of renewal: renewed hope, renewed hunger, a renewed demand that life be something other than winter. Each new spring a time to forget the hard months before, to remember why a man would want to live in God's great country, why he'd drag himself and his family through the chastising snow, the bitter wind that coursed through hollers like constant cannonfire, the dogs howling in back yards with their feet jammed down into the drifts. When spring comes in Appalachia, all is made clear: this is the reason. This is the reason.

He sits on the edge of the platform and looks over the valley. The short wings of a hawk caught in a shear. A car on some distant highway, like a dustmote blowing across the floor. Now and then the wind kicks up and rolls over the bluff, loud as a train. He closes his eyes and leans against the shack. He is hungry. Exhausted. No small part of him hopes today will be the day.

If it's here, he says out loud, then let me see it.

So long as nobody talked, their dinners together were quiet. Their mother working in earnest to put good food on the table and the boys spooning it recklessly into their mouths as though it were slop. They ate as soldiers, like they were still afraid to be separate from their weapons too long. Their mother sometimes imploring them to slow down, to stay a while, but she must have understood how disastrous each minute had the potential to be. That Sunday, Anthony decided to show her.

I have a question, he said. Their mother had made chili and the red crust of it gathered in the corners of his mouth. For Tim. Hey, Tim. I have a question.

Tim looked up from his bowl. I'm here for you, brother, he said. It had, by then, become his standard line. Anthony needed help but didn't want it.

How many haircuts did you give over there? Anthony said.

I don't know, Tim said. Maybe none.

None? Anthony said through a mouthful of food. Holy shit! None! And he started laughing, looking at their mother. None, Ma, he said.

Anthony, please, their mother said. Eat your soup.

No gook mucus on your shoes, brother? Anthony said. Not a single drop?

I don't know, Tim said again.

Well it's no fucking wonder I had to do so much work, Anthony said.

Their mother set her spoon down and covered her eyes with her fingers.

You were a better soldier over there than I was, Ant, Tim said. I was scared the whole time.

You're goddamn right I was. And you're goddamn right you were.

You did what you needed to do to protect our way of life, Ant, Tim said. And I didn't.

Anthony sat chewing. Don't fucking patronize me, you fucking cocksucker.

Anthony, please, their mother said. Can we just eat our soup?

His brother stared at Tim across the table. Eyes thin and black. Face pocked with scars. A line of Band-Aids up his arm where he'd taken a razor to his own skin.

It's not fucking soup, Ma, he said. It's chili. Stop calling it soup.

The afternoon air is warm and cool at the same time, and he lets himself sleep for a while with the breeze over his lap. When he wakes, the sun has reddened and inched its way downward toward the horizon. His empty stomach churns. For a second he feels a pressure on his chest, on his lap and the tops of his legs and he thinks of Grace, her way of stretching her bare legs across his in the heat of the day: on the porch, leaning against the rail; on the couch with the TV on. Grace always more comfortable with her body than he has ever been. She took him up, twisted him, lifted him with her fingertips and set him down wherever she wanted him.

But Sadler. He'd nearly forgotten the night before, forgotten how she took her dress off hastily, forgotten her hard body, her damp hair slipping into his mouth when she arched over him. Her lips had tasted of river water. She had worked herself over him with determination, quiet, as though a part of her regretted it all, laid him flat and pushed herself down into him like she wanted somehow to melt their bodies together. Pumping hard against his hips. When it was over, she stretched across him like a blanket and said, for some reason, that she was sorry.

The 1911 digs at the small of his back. He pulls it to his lap and looks down at it, cradles its barrel in his fingertips. Something is wrong. He thinks of Sadler leaving before he woke and suddenly gets it: she had been the signal. Last night was Grace's way of telling him she needed him. Sadler had been sorry because she knew the message she was carrying. He can't believe he missed the signal.

Before he can convince himself not to, he slides the barrel of the 1911 into his mouth and looks across the valley for one more second, his tongue licking the cool metal, the oil on the rail. He snorts back a sob and tries to remember his wife and when he can't and a picture of Sadler flashes before him instead, he pulls the hammer and fires.

Wake

HE WOKE IN THE DRY AIR OF THE HOSPITAL. The room dark except for a constellation of bluegreen lights in the corner, functions of a machine that made small beeping noises. The windowshades open a half-inch. The night behind them trembling and wide. Grace lay sedated in her bed with her chest rising and falling as it had done for twenty-six years. Nothing new, nothing troubling.

He went to the window and peeked through the shades. The room looked over a parking lot. In one corner, a security light flickered rhythmically, like the beating wings of a bird. A fat man leaning against it, smoking. Glancing up in confusion until it winked out completely; afterward, he stood smoking in the dark. Tim could see the red cherry of his cigarette, the sparks when he threw it to his feet.

He wakes in a small clapboard room. A bare bulb on a wire above him, and on the opposite wall a faded bluegreen painting of Jesus Christ. The yellow halo, the dingy white robe. The savior's gaze waiflike and unnerving. He can hear the clamor of children through the wall at his head, their feet thudding on a hardwood floor, their piercing laughter. The soft voice of a woman calling after them, adjusting them, gently rearranging their behavior. Someone is cooking meat.

He tries to roll onto his side but his face screams and rages. He can taste blood, lick the crust of it from his teeth. He probes with his fingertips and finds his jaw wrapped in gauze, tacky from bleeding. There is a divot in the thick of his cheek. He runs his tongue over a swollen ridge on the inside.

Good thing you're an awful shot, Wiley says. He stands in the doorway with a tray of food. One of his children has her arms wrapped around the great bulk of his leg.

Tim isn't sure he can speak. He works his jaw gently but it doesn't much want to move.

I'm trying to think of a way to get this in you, Wiley says. He sets the tray on a table under the window and drags a chair to Tim's bedside. I'm thinking we tilt you thataway, and I sort of spoon it into your good cheek. What do you think?

What is it, Tim says. His voice thick with spit, his every word a whisper from the side of his mouth.

It's cream of potato soup. A little applesauce. My wife makes her own applesauce. Puts ginger in it. You won't believe it.

I don't know, Tim says.

There ain't nothing chunky in it, Wiley says. I won't choke you.

How'd I get here?

I got boys from up the church like to go rabbit hunting. They was just down in the break, said they seen you go up. When they heard the shot, they knew you were up there and figured the rest for themselves.

The little girl still clinging to Wiley's leg. This is our house, she says.

It is, baby, Wiley says. Hey, run get your mama, will you? Tell her to bring some more wrappings.

The girl looks at Tim for a little too long and bounces away.

Where's my Colt, Tim says.

Oh, ha ha, Wiley says. Yeah, I'm gonna hold onto that for a while. Just for safekeeping. The boys found it in the bramble and wanted to have it, but I said it weren't theirs to have.

It was my daddy's.

Wiley spoons up a bit of soup and waits for him to open his mouth. That right, he says. Well. Now you got this nonsense out your system, let's say you stick around long enough to hand it down again.

Tim grunts. Not interested.

Wiley pulls the spoon back. Well that's a right shame. I might maybe know somebody got big plans for you, once you're all healed up.

Anthony came sometime during the night to sit with him. Tim unable to fall back asleep, his brother had a greasy foil-wrapped sandwich that Tim tore in half. They shared it in the dark, watching Grace's chest rise and fall, rise and fall. Working their fingers gently over the wrapper as if they might wake her.

I believe that beeping would eventually drive a man to violence, Anthony said.

Nighttime. He wakes again. The house is different, quieter. Someone has turned off the light in his room, though a wash of moonlight seeps in through the window and falls across the wall. Jesus' face like a ghost. His halo faded into darkness, his holy hands in shadow. Tim's toes press against the cool iron filigree at the foot of the bed. The frame intended not for him but for a child. He wonders if the little girl at Wiley's hip has given up her mattress for this.

The soreness in his cheek is considerable, though less acute than before. He can turn his head. He can shift his body without suffering a jolt of pain. Gently, he slides his legs to the edge of the mattress and lets them slip off, uses the momentum to sit upright. He waits for a minute with his head dipped and his hands on his knees. His boots tucked neatly under the bed, his bloody shirt nowhere to be found, his pants, his socks. On the desk under the window, a stack of fresh clothes with crisp folded corners.

He dresses quietly, careful not to jostle his face any more than necessary. The pants are too big and the shirt reaches nearly to his knees. He pulls the door open, peeks through. On the far side of the house, a woman sits cross-legged in a rocker with a pile of crochet in her lap. Wiley beside her, reading. Between them a fire burning. The children are nowhere; it must be late. Wiley looks up from his book and motions Tim to come over. Puts his finger to his mouth. Shhh.

He crosses through a small kitchen that still smells of dinner, the rough-hewn floorboards nice on the feet, their crags and splinters worn away by years of family crossings. Smooth and considerable. They remind him of the floors in the farmhouse. At the threshold to the living room the fire's heat hits him in a wave; there must be forty degrees' difference between one room and the next. He slides a chair away from the small dining table and sits opposite Wiley and his wife.

God, I'm glad to see you intact, Wiley's wife says. Intact, I mean. She smiles awkwardly. Her face is round and pretty; the fire has branded a pink stripe across her forehead. She holds her hands in her lap and puffs out her cheeks.

Tim looks at her in a way he hopes doesn't seem cold.

Oh my gosh, what am I doing, she says. My name's Catherine.

Tim, Tim says. Keeping his mouth thin. The less movement the better.

Wiley told me you'd met? We're both just so glad you're here, and—

I'm sorry, Tim says. Thank you for the clothes. And the. He points at his cheek.

Of course, she says, anybody would have.

I should probably leave, Tim says.

Catherine looks at her husband. I'm not sure that's the best idea for you right now, Tim, she says. You've been through a little something.

I'm not sure what I've been through, Tim says. Don't want to be ungrateful, but I have business.

Your business almost got you killed, Wiley says, resting his book across his leg and leaning forward. That fall you took was forty feet if it was five.

I appreciate that, Tim says.

I don't really think you do, Wiley says. Ask you something: your face hurt?

Yes.

Your ribs?

Little sore.

Your legs?

Little sore.

Belly? Arms? No? Is your jimmy a little sore?

He shakes his head gently. Mainly it's my face.

There, you see? Wiley eases himself back into his chair. Them boys found you split over a rock like a dry skin. How come you can't feel that all over?

Just sleep the night off here, Catherine says. If you still feel like leaving in the morning, obviously we can't stop you.

❦ ❦ ❦

Anthony was there when she died. Snoring in the corner, his head wedged between walls, the sandwich foil balled on the edge of the heater beside him. Tim stood at the foot of her bed, holding his chin, knowing somehow that something would go wrong soon. He watched her chest rise, fall, rise, fall, and then. He pressed the nurse call and when she came in, she looked at Grace and then at Tim and said, Oh, God.

Oh, God, what? Anthony said, waking.

It's over, Tim said.

What is? He looked at Grace. Fuck that. He stood, took Grace's wrist in his fingertips. No, fuck that, he said. Get somebody in here.

The nurse did not know what to do.

Don't get anybody in here, Tim said. In fact, please go away. Both of you. Please go away for a minute.

Anthony made to follow the nurse out, turned. Without her, we don't have a chance, he said.

I know it, Tim said.

❦ ❦ ❦

They spent a few weeks stationed at a mountain outpost in Dien Bien province, a remote tent city that blended so well with the jungle you wouldn't see it if you were standing at the base of the hill. Tim was assigned to the medical shelter, running from one side of the thirty-foot canvas to the other to find things: scalpels, towels, the hand of a nurse who wasn't too busy doing something else. The tent was serviceable, like a cave made modern: electric lights run on a gas generator; heavy green supply crates stacked on the downhill side to simulate a shrapnel break; a refrigerator stocked with antibiotics and beer. On hot days, when especially putrid wounds came in, they could roll up the walls to let clean air blow through.

What most amazed Tim about the field hospital was its silence. The nurses professional and trained, the doctors earnest and skillful. They expected quiet and were accustomed to working in it. But the men: one man came in with a nine-inch sliver of wood embedded in his neck; another had shattered his ankle cliff-diving so that pieces of jagged bone ripped through his skin like pins in a cushion; the worst was the sergeant who had pulled a grenade when he heard footsteps on the path behind him, not realizing one of his men had stepped away to take a piss. When he'd noticed the boy's insignia, the sergeant covered the grenade with his body and tore his belly away to the organs. He'd been awake when he came in, reached his hand to Tim and Tim had gripped it, pulled it to his chest. Well, I'm here, the sergeant had said. They'd neutralized his phosphorous burns and wrapped him the best they could and put him on a helicopter to Saigon. Disasters and near-disasters daily things, but the tent always quiet. The men coming in with incinerated skin and holes shot through their lungs and toes popped by stray mines never made a sound. They knew help would come to them in due time. They knew a nurse would hold their hand if they wanted her to. They just kept their mouths shut, pain bearing their lips together, and waited their turn.

He opens his eyes and he's back in the child's bed. Catherine sitting beside him, working the tips of her crochet needles in the soft light of a table lamp. She smiles when she sees that he's awake.

Shhh, she says. I gave you a little something to take the edge off.

What was it?

Just some aspirin.

I'm tired.

I bet you are. All that asking your body to do something it's not meant to do.

What's that?

Quit.

Men

HE THOUGHT HE SAW DEAN GOODELL ONCE, in a second-hand furniture store in Virginia.

He and Grace had spent a long weekend in Chincoteague, eating raw oysters in dive joints and lying around on the beach pretending to read books they couldn't pay attention to. The thick cloud of mosquitoes that seemed perpetually to hover over the island had nearly driven them home early, but they decided instead to lie in their motel room on the last day with the door and windows sealed and their clothes on the floor. When they left, the bed was thrashed as though an animal had feasted there. They hadn't turned the TV on once.

It was early August and hot and that last morning they curled around Washington, south on ninety-five, turned west on sixty-four to find lunch in Charlottesville.

I knew a guy from here, he said. Grace pulling him down the street: she'd seen a sign for barbecue.

She said, Who?

Guy named Goodell. From the war. Funny fucker. Deserter.

People actually deserted?

Not many. It wasn't an easy place to get away from.

They ate at a table in the window and watched people on the street.

My granddad's gonna give us the house, she said.

It was the first Tim had heard of it. *His* house?

She laughed. Yeah, his house. The farmhouse.

For free? Just give it to us? The land, too?

Yes.

How long have you known?

She had barbecue sauce on her lips. Couple weeks.

He smiled. He couldn't think of anything that would make him happier than living in the cut.

I thought you'd be happy, she said.

I am. It's just awfully generous.

Well, she said. Don't give him too much credit. He only barely knows he's doing it.

After lunch they went to the furniture store and that's where he saw Dean Goodell. Wearing a shirt and tie, a brown name tag that Tim couldn't read. There were several customers and Goodell wandered among them, lightly prodding, being a salesman. Some paused to ask him questions; others turned him politely away. Then he looked at Tim, the two of them locking eyes for a second, and Tim thought he saw Goodell's teeth. Goodell made a face as though he'd suddenly remembered something and disappeared into the back room.

I was hoping they'd have a little rocker, Grace said. But no such luck. She'd found a couple of small things: a green ashtray, a knit pillow that looked in good condition. Let's get these and get back on the road.

Tim staring at the back door.

Grace said, You alright?

Yeah, he said. Thought I saw somebody.

The house in the woods was a good place to live. A bedroom for each of them; a tiny bathroom for the boys and a larger one for their mother, a small concrete porch in back where their mother smoked and the boys sat watching fireflies. They could close their doors on each other if they saw fit, but they hardly ever did. They ate dinner together most nights at the kitchen table, which was ugly but came with the rent, played Monopoly under the light of a lamp, which was also ugly but also came with the rent. On weekends they scoured the forest for kindling and built small fires in the upturned lid of a charcoal grill.

He and Anthony lived for their summers there: eight of them before war, eight groups of days blended into one day, time spent sooty and scratched and skinned and soaked. They worked for years on a fort that spanned a shoulder of hillside as wide as a football field, a broad citadel complete with covered passageways and a working catapult, a tower from which they could see the roof of their house a quarter mile away. All of it built with scraps bummed from neighbors, dragged across cornfields during the year and piled near the site until needed. Their project well-known in the area: now and then their mother would pull into the driveway and a neat stack of pulled fencing would be waiting next to the garage, a few old windows rescued from a barn, flooring from a flooded cabin, hubcaps, a coiled hawser, an outhouse door. Tough men in brutal trucks, smiling as they rumbled up, cracking jokes with Tim and Anthony while they unloaded their scraps and relived, for a minute or two, their own boyhoods. The brothers had a rule to use everything they were given.

One morning they crossed the switchback trail worn into the hillside by the soles of their sneakers and sat eating bologna sandwiches on a wooden berm that jutted from the side of the fort, their legs dangling twenty feet into open air—a private feat of engineering they reveled in especially, happy to be the only people alive who knew of it. Anthony with a small sack in his lap and when they finished their sandwiches, they threw the crusts into the woods and he pulled out a framed photo of their father. Wrapped in plastic film, which warped the image slightly.

I thought this place could use a name, Anthony said.

Tim didn't say anything. He looked at their father and knew who it was but also didn't recognize him. It had only been three years.

I was thinking Fort Philip, Anthony said. Castle Phil, maybe.

Castle Phil is stupid, Tim said.

Fuck you, too.

Well. It is.

Alright, then, Anthony said. Fort Philip, I christen thee. He tapped the wall behind him.

Tim said, Just don't call it that in front of Mama.

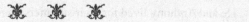

❦ ❦ ❦

A man stands in the room with his back turned: a vest, polyester slacks, hair tapered short at the neckline. Tim can smell his cologne: something meant to attract animals, or people who act like animals.

You're awake, the man says.

I'm awake.

How's your pain?

Tim works himself onto his elbows. Hurts like hell, he says.

McIntire turns. He's bigger than he'd seemed before, when the height of others had tempered his own; his shoulders are broader, his face leaner and sharper at the chin. His jawline shining from a fresh shave.

Reverend, Tim says.

Timothy, McIntire says. He's handsome, in a way: the stiff jaw, the blue eyes those of a psychopath. So, I'm going to try and put this as well as I can. I think you can see we have ourselves something of a problem.

Yeah, I was aware.

As though he hasn't heard him, McIntire says, Now, a problem is not necessarily a bad thing. A problem can help us understand ourselves better in the solving of it. Show us what we're made of, so to speak.

Tim nods, watches McIntire walk to the window and look out.

Still, other problems are buds that just need to be nipped. The kind of thing that's better not to wrestle with too long, lest one become inundated by it. Surrounded, you know, caught up in its tentacles. McIntire holds his hands up as though he's choking someone. Drinking, you could say, is this kind of problem. Gambling is this kind of problem. Drugs. Sex. Better to quit these things fast, and to quit them cold turkey.

Alright, Tim says.

I'm worried about you, McIntire says.

You're wondering which kind of problem I'm having.

No, Timothy, McIntire says. He steps close to the bed, kneels, looks Tim in the face. I'm wondering which kind of problem you *are*.

Anthony tacked the picture of their father to one of the corridor walls, made a show of touching it whenever he walked by. Never moved it. It sat vigil over Fort Philip through rain and hail, the wind that came across the hillside like a wildcat's claws; it faded in the sun and took a grayscale pallor when the snow fell. As far as Tim knew, it watched over their domain while Tim and his brother were in Asia. As far as he knew, it was watching over the fort on the day he'd married Grace. As far as he knew, Philip watched over the fort still, and would forever. Archaeologists might one day uncover the bones of their great city and learn new and exciting things about its civilization, this primitive people eking out their livings such a short journey from a land of modernity and plenty; they would find the photograph of their father and think him a king. They would study the rusty nails, the rotted berm dangling over so much open forest, and wonder how the inhabitants had perished.

It simply couldn't have been Goodell. Goodell was too planning, too careful; he wouldn't have been so foolish. Even when he'd slipped out of his boots in the jungle and sloshed through water until the trench foot was so bad they had to send him for treatment, even that had been a plan. To make himself seem crazy, to dampen any impact when he walked away. To become a lesser asset and not worth chasing. Still, the army knew Goodell had history in Charlottesville. There were people there who knew him, had taught him in biology class, girls there who'd slept with him. Even the laziest investigator would have thought to ask around. He wouldn't have been dumb enough to come home.

But. The fellow at the furniture store had looked just like him. Right down to the beard, and like bound feet will give a child a crooked walk, like rickets will bow the legs, there's a certain hunch a man can get from a year of ducking sniper fire. The guy at the furniture store had gone to the back, and when he went through the door, Tim could clearly see the hunch. He knew it, of course, because he had it himself.

Let me show you something, McIntire says.

Wiley has joined them in the room, and Catherine, who's brought a tray of fresh wrappings, a small mirror, a glass of water.

McIntire holds the mirror to Tim's face. What do you see?

Tim looks at himself for a minute. The bandages soaked through. Brown specks of blood on the exposed part of his cheek, the bridge of his nose, his earlobe.

I see violence, he says. The pain in talking is sharp and furious.

What else?

Exhaustion.

What else?

I don't know, Tim says. I don't know what I'm looking for.

Conviction, McIntire says. You're looking for conviction. It's found in the eyes. Look at your eyes. Do you see anything?

The eye closest to his wound is red, the skin around it swollen and bruised. I see a busted blood vessel, he says.

Do you see any conviction?

Tim hands the mirror back. I wouldn't know.

Sure you would, McIntire says. Let me ask you something, Timothy. You were a soldier, right?

I was.

And how often did you handle a weapon, being a soldier?

Every day.

And how often did you fire it?

More than I wanted to.

And how often—really *think*, now, son—did you miss?

Tim pulled the hammer, blasted a can and watched it flip across the surface of the pond like a caught fish.

Almost never, he says.

Show him, please, Catherine, McIntire says.

Catherine picks the tape from Tim's jaw and gently pulls the wrapping away. What's beneath it is atrocious: a long stitch from the center of his cheek up the side of his head to the center of his ear. His skin blackish purple and pruny. Catherine has done well in cleaning it, the suture seems good, but she can't have helped the truth: that for a split second his skin had been on fire, that it had expanded and contracted fast enough to gape open, the muscle underneath bulging and torn.

Catherine was a nurse, McIntire says. That's how come the stitching is so clean. You'll be fine. He smiled and the corners of his mustache flared. Still, I think you should come by the church later. Wiley'll walk with you, won't you, Wiley?

The big man nodded.

Good, good, McIntire said. Yeah, it'll be nice. Maybe we'll have us some of our own brand of conviction. You just never know.

Conviction

HE SAT SMOKING WITH HIS MOTHER on the concrete slab behind her house. It was early summer, the first fireflies roaming the damp evening air. A world of them, their beacons weaving in and out of the trees, all the way up the hill like stars. Distant campfires on the trail to a holy war. Somewhere up there, in the shadows of a fast-moving world, rested Fort Philip: the defiant skeleton, the old man on arthritic knees, which they couldn't have known had kept them alive those eight summers of days. They couldn't have known how badly they needed something to do with their hands, that their shabby garrison had given them reason enough not to crush each other's throats.

Remember when you boys used to spend all day up there, his mother said.

I was just thinking the same thing.

The cigarettes had eaten all the way to her core; her laugh came out hoarse and whiny. I got a lot of reading done in the summers, she said. Vacuumed the carpet until I cut runs in it.

Yep. That was good times.

My God, no it wasn't! I was so bored, Timmy. And sad? Jesus Christ.

You made a tough decision, Mama.

She blew her smoke away from her son's face. Your daddy made all the decisions for mc that I was ever going to make. Moving out here was just the final word in a long argument that you don't need to know nothing about.

I know about it, Mama.

She looked at him, his war-torn face, his crumbled self-esteem, and back out into the woods. You're a good boy, Timmy. But you don't know shit about shit.

❦ ❦ ❦

It's been long enough since he walked any distance that his legs are loose and unsteady beneath him. Wiley stoops to hoist him and he can smell the big man's tang, the meat on his breath, the sharpness of his body.

Well, Wiley says. You look purty good for a dead man.

I feel like shit.

Wiley frowns at the curse. His little girl wedged into the A-frame between his legs.

Sorry, Tim says.

They leave the girls behind and cross the damp grass in a budding afternoon heat. A few dozen yards up the path he remembers loosely how to walk, though his head is still throbbing and woozy, and begins to put one foot in front of the other.

I been meaning to ask you, Wiley says. Puffing and churning like a train up a mountainside. Why go all the way up the fire tower for a thing like you done? Whyn't just sit on the porch of that old house up there and do the business?

Tim is moving slowly, which seems to suit Wiley just fine. Maybe there's no reason, he says.

Oh, come on, now. Gotta be a reason for something like that.

Catherine seems like a good woman, Tim says.

Wiley stops in his tracks and looks at Tim as though he's been threatened. Blows his long hair away from his eyes with an upturned lip. He carries so much the look of a bull anxious to restrain itself.

She's the woman against which all other women should be judged. Why do you say that?

What if cancer got her?

That's a hell of a question.

I hope it never comes to it, Tim says. Still. What if?

Well, Wiley says, what day of the week would we be talking about?

Does it matter?

Sure it matters.

Today, then, Tim says. Is it Wednesday? He doesn't know how long he's been sleeping.

It is.

Then say it's a Wednesday.

Wiley starts walking again, overtakes him, charges ahead. Says—into the open woods, as though someone else is listening—In that case, I'd go to church. Any other day, I'd go on down to work.

❦ ❦ ❦

The morning his brother left out, Tim had the flu. He'd spent the entire night retching over the commode, and when their mother woke him before daybreak, he stumbled from his room in his bare feet and underwear. His stomach sore from the clenching, his mouth sour. He stood in the hallway and watched Anthony haul his bag up onto his shoulder. Hair wiry and long and down in his eyes, Anthony's biceps bulged in his shirtsleeves and his big feet rolled out in front of him in old sneakers. Tim could smell the cheap aftershave, the aerosol deodorant, the alkaline signature of a teenage body in distress—as teenage bodies so often are. Living out the last real moments of life as he'd known it, what Anthony resembled more than anything was a man in a child's skin, as though his body—his muscles, his jawline, his long fingers—had outpaced its covering, and now the skin had reached its breaking point, giving him the strained, retracted look of a werewolf *de profundis*.

Take care of Mama, he said, and clapped Tim on the shoulder. His strong hand sent a shock through Tim's tender bones. Then Anthony walked out of the house, threw his bag in the backseat of their mother's car, and sat in the front with his head against the window.

Go back to bed, their mother whispered.

I won't sleep.

Well, that makes three of us. But I think you should try.

He watched them back down the driveway and down the road until he couldn't see their taillights anymore and shuffled into Anthony's room and turned on the light. Stood in the doorway drinking his brother's remnants: the track and field medallions tacked above his bed; a small collection of books lined on the floor against a wall; the dented, rusty target cans he'd fished from the pond and carried with him ever since, stacked in a pyramid on the windowsill. Their bullet holes mostly Tim's handiwork. He sometimes wondered if Anthony had been proud of his brother's truth with firearms or had kept the cans as a means of self-motivation. Anthony had little to show for it—there was certainly no linger of a girl's perfume in his bedroom when he left, no banded life savings in a drawer—but he'd always become good at the things he'd set his mind to. If the army gave him enough ammo he'd be the best shot they'd ever seen by the time he left basic training.

Tim turned out the light and flopped down on Anthony's bed. The sun was coming up. The orange glow of it soft through his blinds. He knew he'd see his brother again, though this followed no clear logic and was not supported by any evidence. After all, in a few months, Anthony would step into the mud of the most dangerous place on earth. The most violent place. By then, though, Tim thought, his brother would be quite dangerous himself. He'd be quite good at violence.

❧ ❧ ❧

If he hadn't known the things that had happened since, he'd think he'd returned to the same scene on the same day: the beautiful sky broken wide over the roof of the church, the great green lawn on the hillside knob, the children barefoot, as they seemed to always be. He can hear their whoops and hollers in the trees, understands how it is the girl Sadler has become so good at navigating a forest. The same bulbous women milling in their oversized dresses. The same men, straight as rails except for that particular bit of spine that curves at the base of the neck. McIntire stands on the porch, where it seems he's destined to stand, greeting his people, acknowledging them, collecting their praise and easing their grievances. When he sees Tim, he smiles, quickly, and turns back to his congregants.

This afternoon the band begins with something more subdued, a song that isn't a song at all. The guitarist with the skinny mustache strums a chord for what seems like forever until his bandmates, one by one, jump in. Bass. Fiddle. Drums. The singer, dressed today as though she'd had little time to leave her house—no jewelry, no makeup, her hair in a loose, scrappy ponytail—opens her mouth and moans, her pitch rising and falling, her butt leaving its seat and coming back down again, over and over, until finally the drummer snaps a rimshot on his snare and they all pull to attention: *Hallelujah*, the singer shouts, *Dear Lord, we're comin!*

The churchgoers stand and bounce and wave their hands in the air. The old folks more stiffly, the young folks reckless and half-blind. The band has ripped into something that sounds like "Johnny B. Goode" with different lyrics:

Down in West Virginia where the air is clean
Jesus gave them everything they'd ever need
The mountains and the rivers—they could live their dream
As long as they were citizens of Cal-va-ry.

The lyrics are amateurish, but they undeniably seem a band transformed: the drummer more confident, the guitarist loud and gritty. The singer leaves her seat and claps her hands together above her head. At one point Tim looks down and sees that he's tapping his foot.

You like it, someone says into his ear.

He turns to find Sadler behind him, dancing, clapping.

They do this song every Wednesday, she says, leaning close to shout into his ear. It's a tradition.

He offers a thumbs up. The music pulses through his skin, burns when it reaches the wound across his face.

She points at his bandages and makes a face to ask if it hurts.

I missed, he yells.

At least there's that, she says.

One evening in the last week of Tim's deployment, they camped on the banks of the Dong Nai. A quiet night, nothing much had happened for days. Tim trying to keep his head down so he could bring it home with him. Maksik and Burns leaned on opposite sides of the same tree, whittling pikes from durian wood, sharpening them to aggressive points.

Always gotta have a last resort, said Maksik, who carried an M1 carbine, a .38 caliber Smith & Wesson revolver, a rusty 1911, a switch-blade knife, a thick-handled Buck knife, and a length of metal cord for strangling.

What's your last resort nowadays, Burns said.

Maksik held his arm out to show him the durian pike. Stick this in his fucking eye, he said.

I got you, Burns said. That'll do it.

Somebody had a radio and played it low from his tent. The men lay around, sucking on their hunger, whistling, letting the warm dampness of the jungle settle across their chests like quilts. Some of them played draw with a waterlogged deck, some sat obsessively combing their hair, as though Tina Louise might emerge fully-formed from the swamp, tired from her journey and looking for a good man to warm her.

The hissing started just as the sun was going down. Like air from a tire, but close, angry.

The fuck is that, Burns said, sitting up.

Sh, sh, Maksik said.

Zip calls, Burns said.

Fuck you, zip calls, Maksik said. That's a croc.

A croc?

Shut the fuck up, Burns. Maksik stood slowly and the rest of them stood, too, on instinct. Sizemore, at the edge of their perimeter, pulled his sidearm. Tim shouldered his M1.

The beast's tail flashed through the fallen leaves on Tim's side of camp, thrashing underbrush like a tiny storm, and then there she was, charging directly at him, a black demon of gaping mouth and wild eye. Tim stumbled backward, flipping the safety on his weapon and tried to aim, but she was quick, invisible even, and he was afraid of shooting someone behind her and so he didn't fire. Thought of the sergeant at the field hospital in Dien Bien, figured this monster might well be his phosphorous grenade: *Eat me, and not these men.* But then the softbelly's body stopped with a jerk and Tim looked up to see Maksik holding her by the end of the tail, leaning with all his strength to pull her away, and when she turned to look at him, Maksik leapt onto her back and drove his freshly-sharpened pike into the valley of skin between her eyes.

They gathered around the animal's body and bowed their heads. Maksik had forced the stick all the way through her jaw and out the bottom and pinned her to the ground. Her blood pouring into the dirt. Maksik on her back, panting.

Jesus Christ, Tim said.

You were in a bad spot, Burns said. I wanted to tell you to set still so he'd leave you alone.

They made a fire and Maksik decapitated her and peeled off strips of her skin with his Buck knife and they roasted it on sticks. In the morning they left her body behind and walked off into the jungle with the stink of roasted flesh on their fingertips.

Serpents

McINTIRE LEANS DEEPLY INTO THE LECTERN and looks over his parishioners. Their pink faces and damp hairlines. Licking beads of sweat from their lips and adjusting their clothes like post-coital teenagers.

The Spirit is here today! McIntire says. Whoo boy, is it ever! Just *look* at you people! Look at you!

They turn and greet each other, still panting from the music, smiling, happy to be alive. It's true: the energy inside Calvary Church of Jesus is different than it had been before. The air thinner and livelier in the lungs. The windows up and a generous breeze blowing in from across the field: the smell of cut grass and earth and honeysuckle. After a short sermon McIntire turns and whirls his hand and the band starts up again. As though a new electricity has taken hold of them. They are full of juice. The guitarist makes strained faces and the drummer hammers the snare like he's beating an animal away. At one point the singer sets down her microphone and lets loose and her voice caroms free along the ceiling like a housefire.

Tim turns back to Sadler. She stands calm and straight-backed, an anomaly against the gyrating mass of churchgoers. A lighthouse in a hurricane. She smiles at him and her eyes are big and hopeful. She is wide-open.

If he has wondered yet what purpose it serves to come along to this place, this church, the question no longer really moves him.

Grace's aspirations had been everywhere and nowhere at once.

I think I want to go to Niagara Falls, she'd say. Her face wistful, her fingers drawn to her chin. But it's really just a big bathtub. Why would that be? Why would I want go all that way to see a big bathtub?

Not sure, Tim said, distracted by whatever.

Maybe I should get a magnifying glass and go turn our faucet on. Same experience, or not the same experience?

You never know until you try.

Impossible to tell if she was testing him. Impossible to know what she thought about Niagara Falls, or Acapulco, or Las Vegas, or anywhere. She was always so happy and so restless.

Standing naked in the bathroom with a hair dryer, she'd say, Who needs a beach breeze? Could you just wave this over me for a few minutes?

He was so scared of disappointing her. So scared that he'd never be able to give her all the things she wanted, all the things she deserved. His only wish to serve her well, to serve her long, to put enough rope together that one day he might lasso for her a star. And then.

Maksik had peeled away what skin he could from the crocodile's skull and cinched the jawbone to his pack and there it hung, a talisman warning followers not to come too close, leftover bits of flesh brown and reeking against the bone, shrinking and expanding with sun and rain like living tissue. Once, Tim found himself behind Maksik in formation, staring at the croc's eyesockets, awed at the nonchalance with which Maksik bore the defining feature of an animal that had tried to end Tim's life. Maksik had popped the eyes out with his thumbs and chucked them into the deep forest.

Your buddy's starting to stink, Burns told Maksik. Flies are getting to him.

Shut the fuck up with that buddy stuff, Maksik said, pointing backward with his thumb. This here's a guardian angel.

Maksik kept an assortment of guardian angels in the jungle: a broad hopea leaf, singed around the edges, that he'd picked up after a firefight and tied to his helmet (all but disintegrated now but its brown stem still hung from a bit of string); a pair of shoes a village girl had given him (in exchange, she must have assumed, for the lives of her family members), which hung from his pack not far from the croc's gaping maw; the enormous python skin that he'd worn at his chest like an after-party necktie. The fact that he was still alive, Maksik said, was proof enough of his angels' power, and fuck all of you boys who wish they had something better to believe in.

The snakes come out in a rush after McIntire has finished his sermon. Tim is not looking and then he is, and several men near the front of the room have their upraised hands woven through the coils of tight brown bodies. Released from their holding cages, the animals take in their new environment with what seems like mere curiosity: they move slowly down the arms of their handlers; they jut forward from hands and over the open air, stiff as tree branches. Their tongues flitting like boys learning to stab. McIntire takes one from someone and the snake immediately begins to twist around his head, running its scales over the preacher's face with the gentleness of a woman, the tiny head resting beside his ear as though ready to tell him a secret. Tim is vaguely aware that the band is pulsing in the background, that people are dancing, that the pain in his jaw has faded. He watches McIntire dance between his people, possessed. His cheap shoes and damp button-down, locks of hair licking his face, bulbs of thick yellow sweat on his lip. The preacher turns his dirty fingers through the snake's knots, splitting them, curling them, giving the animal places to focus its energy.

My God, someone beside Tim says.

A few seats down, a woman collapses into the aisle. No one moves to help her. She kneels on all fours for a moment, her spine arching like a cat's, pulls her dress from under her knees and wraps it around her waist, looking for all the world like a woman enjoying an act of sex; then she rolls onto her back and spreads her arms and legs and pinches her face together and her tongue begins to flip in and out of her mouth like those of the snakes dangling above her head.

The Spirit, someone shouts.

The Spirit, someone else says.

Haw rat a tamba, the woman shouts. Aw rist a ma taw ba, caw rat a taborah.

The churchgoers stand around her in a circle, dancing, their arms raised, unconcerned about the pain she may or may not be in. Tim watches her flailing. She reminds him, more than anything else, of a woman being burned alive.

❦ ❦ ❦

He never took her anywhere, largely because he never wanted to go anywhere himself. He gambled that the cut would be enough, that to step onto the porch in the red-orange mornings and breathe the sweet air rolling down from the forest, that to leap from their flat stone jutting out above the creek into cool brown water and emerge anew, was preferable to any great wall, to any dusty trench in the earth, to any spire reaching rusted and clunky toward the heavens. He gambled that stillness would win out over chaos. If he'd had his way, within a couple of years they'd have a garden acre, suckling pigs and a stout brood of chickens and a cow or two for milk, the radio, a shelf of secondhand books, and little reason left over to leave. They'd have their child and raise him at home, give him the Appalachian earth as his plaything, the Appalachian sky as his blanket. They would teach him to read and to fish, to multiply and to trap, to inquire and to tie a half-hitch. If Tim had his way their little family would slowly melt down into the mountains, would camouflage itself against the detritus on the forest floor until the individual members were barely recognizable as human, and if someone from town had met one of them by pure and unavoidable accident there would be no way to tell where the person ended and the country began. If Tim had his way they would pack together like bears, roaming the forest for morsels and places to scratch their backs; they would perch in tall trees like eagles watching over their dominion; they would weave amongst dead things on the ground, copperheads bearing a healthy mistrust of the outside world, a charge of perfect venom, the undeniable pattern of decay drawn cleverly across their skin.

McIntire steps into the crowd with a snake balanced awkwardly on his shoulder. He eyes Tim excitedly, as though he's lost his mind, left it behind somewhere, and his body is being propelled forward by something other than his own will. No one reaches to touch the animal, but neither do they shy from it. They clap their hands and bend their knees and the band plods on happily. Wiley has taken some room beside the lectern and stands with his arms outstretched and his eyes closed, a giant smile on his oversized face. At his arm a beautiful young woman that could be his dead wife gyrates with the grace of a heavy snowfall, her dress twisting and billowing with the energy in the atmosphere. Tim blinks, and when he looks at her again, Mama McIntire has taken her place and is staring back at him with her socket eyes, clasping her brittle fingers and bent stiffly on arthritic knees.

The house is full. Packed to its gills with celebrants in their reverie. Its walls swelling outward. He can feel their warm sweaty crush on his shoulders, leaning into him like drunks outside a bar; their breath, their underarms, their overloud voices speaking things barely discernible into his ear. He has the sudden feeling that he's become one of them, and rather quickly: last time, they'd looked at him slant, questioned everything about his being and about his presence; this time they closed in on him with the abandonment of lovers, their slick skin rubbing against his own, their tongues whispering ludicrous things and leaving the spittle drying across his neck. As though they're drawn to his wound. As though his sudden show of weakness endears him somehow to their pack.

McIntire presses down the aisle and Tim feels a commotion behind him. People are gasping, crying out in voices of joy: Praise Him! Thank Jesus and the Holy Spirit! Praise the Lord! And when he turns, he sees Sadler with her arm outstretched and a full-grown copperhead slithering away from her father's hands and onto her own pale, taut skin. She appears taken by some euphoria, her eyelids fluttering and her lips yammering words in no language he's ever known. He looks at McIntire and sees in the preacher's face something he recognizes from scant recollections of his own: the picture of pride his father had worn that day at the pond, with the bullets and the beer cans; the picture of faith that his mother had bravely painted on herself the morning she drove her eldest son to basic training, knowing she'd never see the same person again, even if he somehow managed to get out of the thing alive.

Lambs

EARLY ONE SUMMER his crew was hired to paint Victory Cinemas, the two-screen movie house where, years before, his brother had made out with Heather Coffee. It was a big project: the theater's new owners, middle-aged expats from Manhattan, wanted it done inside and out, head to toe, and had from the outset made their demanding natures known. Walter, the stern, barrel-chested husband, would follow behind and inspect for drips and splatter on the carpet, while his wife, Natalie, a milky, far-fetched beauty, went from dropcloth to dropcloth peering into paint cans as though choosing a soup to eat. Nervous parents with a new baby, the outside world still more of a threat to their delicate progeny than a comfort.

On a sunny afternoon Tim was on a ladder edging around the marquee. Natalie somewhere beneath him, in scrutiny either of his work or of his backside. Either way welcome to do as she pleased: let her worry over her investment or let her have her fun; neither were likely to rile him much on a day as beautiful as it was.

Tim, he heard her say from below, though he hadn't given her any reason to know his name.

Help you, Missus Reynolds?

Watch yourself coming, she said.

He ducked to look down the street at a gaggle of schoolchildren walking toward them, holding hands and singing. He climbed down and stood with his arms folded, brush tucked across an elbow, and smiled at the kids when they passed. He looked for Grace, who'd gone in to substitute that day, but the teacher at the end of the line was a small, balding fellow who smiled proudly and tapped a yardstick on the ground as he went by.

Good day for a walk, the teacher said.

That it is, Tim said.

Sorry to make you stop, Natalie said, once the children were gone.

It's alright. It's good judgment.

She smiled and looked down at several flowering drops of paint on the sidewalk. Just wouldn't want anyone anointed who wasn't ready to be, she said, and he noticed for the first time a golden crucifix hanging between her breasts. He'd assumed, for no reason at all, that she was Jewish.

❦ ❦ ❦

One day you'll be an old man, Maksik had told him, and you'll have gone crazy. You'll spend your days on a rickety porch with a cup of instant coffee. You'll have a dog with a stupid name by your feet. Sweetie. Pudding. You'll be alone, because everyone you ever knew and loved will have left you. Too painful to watch you rot.

They sat at the edge of a grass flat, smoking cigarettes and watching stars push through the thin film of the sky.

You'll have a favorite game show host, that's how fucking lame you'll be, Maksik continued. You'll read the same books twice because you can't remember the first time you read them. He took a draw from his cigarette. It'll be twenty-five years since you even *thought* about a slice of pussy—and forty since you had any.

It was the last day of Tim's tour and they were waiting for the huey to come pick him up and lift him out of the shit. He was distracted, and the point of the conversation had passed Tim by. Maksik projecting his own future forward, maybe, giving it someone else's name so he needn't be quite so scared of it.

And then, one day, you'll remember you were a man once, Maksik said. You'll remember you once wielded a mighty weapon, a fire stick that gave you the right to decide futures, and that you'd used it valiantly in a campaign against other men. Men with brains. Men with dicks and lovers and drug habits and ideas, just like you. Men who liked a dirty joke. Men who loved their mamas. That you'd pointed it and fired it and turned other men's heads into canoes.

Tim wasn't sure he'd ever turned anyone's head into a canoe.

And then you'll think, Hey! I could do it all over again, couldn't I? Wage one more hateful campaign, but this time I'm a one-man army with a single enemy! How hard could it be?

He'd looked at Maksik, at the shadow of the man's head, the orange light from his cherry cast across his mustache. What the fuck are you talking about, he said.

Somewhere in the blackness, the whumping of chopper blades.

You're now the proud owner of memories you'll never want, Maksik said. Memories you aren't gonna shake. You'll be looking for a remedy.

I hope it never comes to that.

Me too, but it will. And when it does, you'll remember the talk we had here today.

❧ ❧ ❧

He has to see her. He's borne witness to something he can't understand and needs somebody who knows about it to explain. Like the first time a child sees a man with no legs, a picture of a woman spreading herself open, footage of a snake swallowing a deer. He needs Sadler to tell him why nobody is dead.

He waits in the yard while the congregants file out. Some glance and smile. Others ignore him and make twisted faces at their spouses. Their engines rumble and sputter as they wind their various ways down the mountainside.

After some time, Wiley steps onto the porch and raises his meaty hand in greeting. Got an elders' meeting, he says. We'll be a while yet. You want to, head on back to the house and get you something to eat. Catherine's making chicken and dumplings. He turns and opens the screen door and steps back inside.

When he's alone and the blue light of dusk has risen over the treetops and the crickets begin their whirring, he realizes he could have asked someone for a ride to anywhere. Could have been down off the mountain in a half hour, at a payphone, a diner.

Wiley still has his father's pistol.

He watches the door for what feels like forever, but Wiley does not come back out. Neither does Sadler, McIntire, or Mama.

❧ ❧ ❧

Grace's grandfather went into the nursing home having neglected to tell them one of his ewes was pregnant. Tim had assumed the grimy beasts were too decrepit for such a thing; to look at them you'd think the old man had showed them nothing but contempt for all the years of their lives. It turned out Tim's town-boy mental image had just been queer: sheep are filthy as pigs, filthier even, their belly hair matted with turds and mud, their fleece stained yellow by weather and grease. Much work goes into nice, white, knitting wool. More than seems sane. A wonder the idea of it ever became reality at all. Anyway. One of the foul creatures was indeed with child, and Tim and Grace unwittingly found themselves midwives in a rainy season of scouring cold. They hardly knew how to dress for the occasion, much less how to assist in the birthing of a live animal.

Gary, the gym teacher at Grace's school and a fourth-generation farmer, had given her the advice to let nature run its course. Best not to intervene.

God's been at this since the world began, he'd told her.

Well, Grace had said. We wouldn't know how to intervene if we wanted to.

That may be just the ticket, then, Gary said. You can call me if you run out of options. He gave her a slip of paper with his telephone number on it.

She'd smiled and tucked it into her purse.

And now here they were: Thursday night in the middle of nowhere, light sucked away by the vindictive tail end of winter, and the ewe, whom Grace had hastily christened Mama, backed into a corner of her stall, ambling side-to-side on loose joints as though stoned. He wouldn't have admitted it, but Tim felt a welling sense of responsibility for Mama's fortunes; he knew if the ewe didn't survive, or if the lamb was stillborn, he'd manage to blame himself. They'd long been waiting for their sheep to die so they could skip feeding them, but now that it seemed possible they became anxious and regretful.

Grace opened the door gently and slipped into Mama's stall.

Gracie, careful, Tim said.

She's in labor, Grace said. I think I can dodge her if she comes at me.

And indeed, with Grace sitting beside her, the ewe seemed to calm. She quit pacing and lay down on her side and let Grace run her fingers through the wool on her flank. Her breathing slowed. Now and then she would cock her head up, because things were happening inside her that they couldn't control or because she wanted to make sure Grace was still there. Both, maybe.

Mama's labor seemed to take forever. Grace nestled into the straw alongside her, Tim perched on an open ladder with his chin against the door. Now and then Mama groaned softly, like a tired man content in his bed. The air had gotten colder and carried with it the dry tang of a coming snowfall.

Maybe we should call this Gary guy, Tim said.

Grace had closed her eyes and leaned against the wall. Her fingertips buried in Mama's down, scratching gently at the skin below.

What for?

Just taking a while, Tim said.

Let it take a while, then. Gary'll just come over here and scare her.

And then, as though she'd been listening, Mama popped up and groaned and the glistening bulb of her amniotic sac slipped away from her vulva. She began to pace the stall again, more quickly than before, while Grace cooed at her and formed unintelligible words, and several minutes later the front hooves of Mama's lamb shone through, and then its nose, and Tim instinctively moved to catch the animal before it fell to the floor. It wrenched out of Mama's body quickly and he caught it in his cradled hands.

Lay it down, lay it down, Grace was saying. Lay it down with her so she can smell it.

But Tim couldn't make his limbs do what he needed them to do. He sat there on his knees with this new life against his belly, suddenly unsure how to proceed. Grace wicked slime away from the lamb's eyes and nostrils and its softly opening mouth.

My God, Tim had said.

Lay it down with her, Grace said. She needs to smell it.

A single light burns in a side room of Calvary Church of Jesus. Tim leaning against a tree in the yard, watching for comings and goings, his arms crossed against the cold. Now and then he catches himself dozing, wakes and touches the damp gauze on his cheek. The wound is weepy and needs fresh dressing.

Finally, a figure steps into the room and blocks out some of the light. This must be Wiley. He's followed by a procession of smaller folk. The preacher. Sadler. Mama the shape-shifter, whose mere shadow is frail, and who for a moment seems to be looking out the window, directly at where Tim is sitting. For a split second her eyes are bright as flashlights. Then she turns her head and their business proceeds.

You should scoot up, someone says, and Tim slips from his perch against the tree, rolls once into the grass. He looks up and in the new moonlight can barely make out Jonas, the boy from the restaurant with the crooked smile, crouched in the weeds just beyond where he'd been sitting.

Jesus Christ, Tim says. You scared me.

Sorry, Jonas says. He screws up his face as though he might cry. I'm sorry.

Tim sits again and dusts his hands on his knees, points toward the church. You know what this is?

The boy's expression snaps back to one of amusement. He scrambles to a patch of grass beside Tim. It's a bloodbath, he says.

What the fuck, Tim whispers, looking at thc window.

Come on, Jonas says. He grabs Tim by the elbow and pulls him on a wide arc through the yard. They kneel together behind the hood of a rusty brown Oldsmobile.

Mama's car, Jonas says, and swipes at it with his fingertips.

Tim sees McIntire more clearly now, watches him put his hand on Sadler's shoulder, watches her sink to her knees. Wiley has a bucket, and when he sets it down, the preacher dips his hand in and pulls it out dripping with blue-black liquid and smears his fingers quickly across his daughter's face. Mama does the same. Wiley dips a palmful and lays it out over Sadler's hair, and it drips down her cheeks and over the bridge of her nose and into her eyes.

Lamb's blood, Jonas whispers.

Tim turns to him. That's blood?

The boy giggles softly. Yeah.

Jesus Christ.

Kinda, Jonas says.

Reasons

OCASIO HAD NOT HUNG THERE LONG ENOUGH to change color. Tim was surprised by that. He was surprised by the way the men stood silent and gaping around the young man's body as though waiting for his next magic trick. He was surprised by how beautiful the morning had been, how the pink sun had come up over Ocasio's shoulder, how the insane noise of the jungle had died down for a few minutes, that they might look over their friend one more time in peace and imagine themselves somewhere else, somewhere more wonderful, in a place where *wonder* meant nothing more or less than *quiet*.

It is not useful to trouble over a man's motives too long. If he has them at all, he will be reluctant to share, and if he overcomes that reluctance they will be significant only to him. Why Ocasio strung himself up with a pair of belts was not for them to know, in the end. A conversation between the boy and his Creator. But of course there existed in each of them a vast body of evidence, and certainly they all felt a sort of noose around their necks; why Ocasio had chosen to attach it to something mighty and swing from it, and why the rest of them had not, led to a sort of madman's dance, a jaunty thing that loosened the mouth and twisted the legs. You could tell a man who'd succumbed to it by the crazy way he talked, by the way he always appeared to be running from someone whispering in his ear.

If it wasn't their lot to understand Ocasio's motives neither were they to question why Dean Goodell had run away. A crazy fuck, but they were each crazy enough in their own ways. Homesick, maybe, but homesick men came a dime a dozen. No, they would never really know why Goodell had done what he'd done, and they'd never know what it was that had kept them from going with him.

Why do you love me? Grace asked one night. This was when she was still good, still healthy.

What kind of question is that? Your food's getting cold.

She did this. Got distracted by a thought, cradled it in her head, softly, like an egg, turned it and felt it with her fingertips and held it to the light to look for imperfections.

I think it's something I have to know, she said. Anyway, now that I've said it you can't let it just lay there.

He set his fork down on the rim of his plate. Wiped his mouth and mustache, balled the napkin on the table.

What's the question again?

Why you love me, she said. Her face was wide, excited, as though she'd give him a million dollars if he gave her the right answer.

I don't know, Grace, he said, which was a lie; of course he knew. He loved her heart, the size and the weight of it; he loved the smell of her sleeping body; he loved how kind she was to people. He loved that the things he enjoyed—the land, the water, the quiet satisfaction of a day's work—were also important to her, loved that she gave him the room he needed to draw a deep breath, to roam, to pick at his old wounds, and that she was always open when he came back. He loved that she asked him earnest questions like why he loved her, even if he couldn't answer them.

You're beautiful, for starters, he said.

She choked out a laugh. No, I'm not! She ran her fingers through her hair, as though it disproved anything, and swigged the milk in her glass.

And you're a great teacher.

Timothy, she said. I can't even land a full-time job. Be serious.

Fine. Fine. He worked a piece of meat against his jaw, thinking, and said, You're going to make someone an excellent mother.

They were both quiet for a minute. The walls swelled and retreated. Grace with her head turned sideways as though someone had called for her from another room.

Well, okay, Tim said. I love you for all the things you're not, then.

Grace laughed so hard a spurt of milk shot from her nose.

❦ ❦ ❦

We should go, Jonas whispers.

The elders have left Sadler alone in the side room, and Tim can see her wicking the blood from her eyes with her fingers. She scrapes it from her hair and wipes it out of the corners of her mouth.

Yeah, we should go, Jonas says again, and begins to shuffle back toward the treeline. Tim follows, aware suddenly that he's seen something he's not to have seen, that to be found here would not be good for him. They split through the bramble and crouch in a pocket of undergrowth. He searches for Sadler in the soft yellow light, but she's gone.

Hoooo, Jonas says. Just in time. Look.

Wiley and McIntire and Mama come down from the porch and cross the yard and file into their Oldsmobile. The engine whines and stutters and turns over and McIntire flicks on the headlights, two golden circles cast back into the woods. Tim thinks of the light people claim to see just before they die.

Finally, Sadler emerges. Her hair in a ponytail. Her face scrubbed white. She turns to check the door is locked, steps barefoot off the porch and into the grass. Stands for a second looking into the black patch of trees where Jonas and Tim are hiding and Tim thinks he sees her smile. Then she opens the back door of the Oldsmobile and disappears inside.

❦ ❦ ❦

There was a night when he and Anthony came in from the hillside, grubby and speckled with dirt and blood. Construction on Fort Philip was coming along nicely; there was much to show for their labor, despite there being no one they wished to show it to. They left their boots in the doorway and rumbled like called pigs toward the kitchen. On his way past, Anthony bent to flick on the television, though no one ever watched it.

Their mother had made dinner—tuna casserole with French beans and rolls, a perennial favorite—and laid out silverware and filled their glasses halfway with milk. She made it look easy to keep her two wildebeests satiated, though it had to have been anything but; their appetites for everything—food, bloodshed, high school girls and their high school bodies, TV westerns, the sight of themselves shirtless in the mirror—were enormous. Catastrophic, simian. Thoughtless, heedless, endless. Her boys like wild dogs: pissing where they stood, pinning their food to the ground with their feet and gnashing at it with sharp teeth, thrusting their noses into the air to follow the particulate smell of a passing woman's underarms. The only thing she could do was open the back door and trust they'd come in when she whistled.

At the corner of the table, three small plastic-bound books the boys had paid no attention to while they jabbed at the casserole with serving spoons and gritty fingernails.

I stopped by the library today, their mother said. On the way home from work. There was a man by the door handing these out. She gave one of the books to Anthony, one to Tim. I thought maybe we could read them together.

The Holy Bible, Tim said.

Anthony with a cheekful of noodles. The *fuck*, Mom?

Anthony, their mama said. Watch your mouth. You're spitting fish all over. And it's God's word, for crying out loud.

I'm not reading it, Anthony said.

Why not?

Because it's bullshit.

Millions of people can't be wrong, Ant, Tim said, though he didn't want to read the Bible any more than his brother did.

Millions of people are wrong all the time, Anthony said. He stuffed another forkful of food into this mouth and added, It wasn't too long ago that everyone alive thought the earth was flat. It wasn't too long ago that a million Germans thought Hitler was a role model.

That's different, their mama said.

Tim thumbed through the book, rubbing its translucent pages between his fingers, ignoring its words. His food untouched in front of him.

I just thought we could use a little, I don't know, their mama said. A little perspective.

Here's some perspective, Anthony said, and snatched his Bible off the table and walked into the bathroom. A plunk, followed by the sound of the toilet flushing. He came back and sat and bit off half a roll.

Tell me you didn't just do that, their mama said.

It was a bad idea, Mom, Anthony said. I'm sorry.

I thought it would be nice. Please tell me you didn't do that.

It isn't nice, Mom. It's dangerous bullshit. Eat your food.

Before bed that night, Tim went to take a piss and, sure enough, Anthony's little red copy of the Bible sat in a small pool of water in the toilet bowl, like a boulder in a pond. He plucked it out with his fingertips and threw it in the trash.

❧ ❧ ❧

He and Jonas navigate the road by moonlight, the soles of their shoes slouching across the dirt, hands shoved into their pockets. Jonas talks indiscriminately of trivial things. His vocabulary is basic, and he seems mainly to understand the world in terms of fairness and unfairness, the value of actions on a scale of fun and boredom. Like a five-year-old. That, Tim realizes, is essentially what Jonas is: a small boy lurching along in a man's body. He guesses Jonas is fifteen or sixteen, but only by his looks; the kid is otherwise raw and green, new to the world, a sapling unaware of the existence of hailstorms and chainsaws.

Jonas, I have to ask you a question, Tim says, and for the first time in ten minutes the boy is silent. The spring cold has wrapped around them. Whenever they pass under a canopy of overhanging branches, the light goes almost entirely away. Tim says, I need you to tell me about your life here.

They continue on the sloping road for a while, quiet. Fog from their breath winding around their heads.

Jonas?

You said you had a question, Jonas says, and Tim can tell from his voice he's trying not to laugh. I'm still waiting.

Okay, Tim says. What's your life like here, Jonas?

Incredible, Jonas says.

They are close enough to Tim's truck that he can see moonlight glinting from its bumper.

That's it? Incredible?

I do whatever I want, Jonas says. All day long.

You don't go to school?

Until I was seven I did. They told Daddy I was a retard.

Did you never go back after that?

Nope.

Do you think they really said that to your daddy?

He's a preacher. He ain't allowed to lie to me.

It strikes Tim as unbelievable that he'd not understood Jonas and Sadler as siblings. It explains so much: her easy way with the boy that morning at the diner, her casual sympathy for his plight with the peaches, the cool way she disarmed his looming upset. And now that he knows it their resemblance seems undeniable.

Sadler is your sister, Tim says.

Only by half, Jonas says. Dennis is my daddy and her daddy.

But you have different mamas?

Yep. My mama is in Heaven. But Sadler's mama is alive, though. She's called Catherine.

When they reach his truck, Jonas leans against it as though trying to steal residual heat. He puts his cheek against the hood and listens, the backwoods doctor diagnosing a silent pneumonia.

Jonas, Tim says, why did your daddy do that to your sister just now?

The blood?

The blood. Why did they do that?

Jonas straightens and bares his crooked teeth. Because she's a sinner.

Adultery

ANTHONY HAD MANAGED ONE, just one, reasonable relationship with a woman in all the years Tim had been alive. Her name was Celia, and she was the exact opposite of anyone Anthony had any right to get along with: beautiful, responsible, smarter than the two brothers put together. A nurse at KingsHaven, where miners with black lung went to receive their death sentences and then, months or years later, to die. On the weekends Celia wore flowing skirts and bangles on her wrists and let her substantial breasts move as they wished, free from the hindrance of undergarments. She dragged the brothers to the park at Victory Elementary and taught them to throw a Frisbee. When she visited their mama's house, she always brought along a carton of beer. She was funny and excitable and emotional and adamantly anti-war.

You don't belong here, their mama told her the first time they met. The two women had hugged in greeting, recognizing a connection, and now Celia stood barefoot in the kitchen, holding pineapple upside-down cake, smiling with her straight teeth and twinkling eyes. Their mother had crushed her cigarette in the tin plate she kept on the windowsill.

I couldn't agree more, Celia said, and jabbed Anthony in the ribs with her finger. Tim standing off in the corner, gazing on this strange and wonderful creation with nervous interest.

That's Timmy over there, their mama said, forcing Tim out of his trance.

Mama's right, he said, offering his hand. What the hell are *you* doing here?

They all laughed except Anthony. Anthony cast his brother a look that said, *Careful. Careful.*

❦ ❦ ❦

His little world in the trailer is how he'd left it: his father's duffel on the floor, unbothered; the stack of pictures on the chair; his toothbrush on the kitchen counter. This is what they would have found of him after they found his body. This mess of an ending. This filthy, prideless desperation. A life whittled down to its absolute nub by the end of another life. If the bullet had gone through his brain, as intended; if he'd collapsed backward onto the decking as he'd thought he would; if, when they came upon his remains, the wind had been blowing in his hair and at the edges of his clothes; if his eyes had stayed open; if they'd looked upon his face and saw the reflection of the milky sky and the mist of blood that had sprayed upward and caught in the wind and settled back down onto his skin, would anyone among them have understood why this day had finally come? Would they have looked on him with pity, recognizing a man at the end of his capability, and apologized on behalf of the rest of the world for all the things life never managed to provide him?

No, he thinks, standing amongst his scattered belongings. They'd have found his broken, useless body, and later this mess of a farewell, and spit in the dirt at their feet and said, *Jesus Christ*, but not to evoke Him or to curse Him but because His name is what they said when what they meant to say was *Holy shit, get a load of this poor bastard*.

❦ ❦ ❦

His brother was as tortured in love as he was in life. His soul split in two—cleaved, like a beef. The symmetry of his guts spilling from either side of him visible only to those who knew him best and longest. Celia, beautiful as she was, didn't stand a chance: though she'd quickly become a staple of their small family gatherings, and though they came to look forward to her uninhibited laugh and her grass-stained footsoles, and though she'd proven herself a capable cook and a willing participant in late-evening hikes to the ruins of Fort Philip, she was simply never destined to withstand the smell of Anthony's insides.

Grace had been there to witness the truth of the matter. It was a warm summer evening, and the three of them—Tim, his mama, and Grace—sat watching the woods fill up with blackness, the quiet satisfaction of full bellies and several beers apiece, the comfortable knowledge that conversation was unnecessary. Celia tending to Anthony in the back room, where their mama had made up a bed and where Anthony customarily went to sleep off his mistakes: when she finally came out, bare feet padding on the cracked patio stone, her hair high and loose and she struggled to catch a good breath.

Well, then, she said, and it was clear that something in her aura had altered, and that the words that came out over the next hour or so were going to be words of farewell.

Their mama looked at her—this girl who, she'd confided to Tim, she hoped would become her daughter, but who obviously never would; she was destined to be just another valuable thing Anthony managed to break—and wrenched out a smile. How's he feeling?

Not good, Celia said. He's pretty drunk.

Poor baby, their mama said.

Did he eat anything, Grace said, but quietly, as though it wasn't her place. The two of them could have been sisters, Celia and Grace; they certainly bore similar traits. Both lovely, light, the type of shapeshifter who could join any group. The type to be infatuated with life, to drink its milk to the last drop. It occurred to Tim that his brother might have seen a light in Grace that he needed shone on himself, had gone out seeking it, and had, maybe despite the odds, found a reasonable facsimile in Celia.

He ate a hot dog, Celia said, but he couldn't keep it down. She sat for a minute chewing at the tip of her thumbnail. I think I have to ask you guys something.

Anything, Grace said.

How fucked up is he?

Excuse me a second, their mama said. She stood and lit a cigarette and went into the house. The aluminum screen door slammed behind her.

Shit, Celia said. I didn't mean to offend anybody.

She has a hard time talking about it, that's all, Tim said.

Anthony's got a huge heart, Grace said. He loves his mama so much. Hey—the day I met him, actually, I watched him save a snapping turtle's life.

But she stopped talking then. Maybe knowing Celia had no interest in turtles, whether they were dead or alive. They sat listening to the crickets, critters burrowing through dead leaves, the distant wailing pitch of stars streaking across the heavens.

Anthony is the most fucked up human being you'll ever know, Tim said.

❦ ❦ ❦

He pulls everything from the duffel and arranges it on the floor, taps his fingertips on Grace's shirt, riffles the pages of *Slaughterhouse Five*. Then he puts it all neatly back in. The pain in his cheek humming again: it's made an obnoxious habit of letting him free every now and then before returning with a fury. He is hungry, having eaten nothing since Wiley and Catherine's house.

So tomorrow, he thinks. Tonight he will rest and tomorrow he will have one more look at the Ford. If he can't fix it he'll hike his way back down the mountain and find a way to get home. He can't imagine what he'll do after that. Set the house afire and lie on their bed and wait it out. Sit on the flat rock at the creek and starve. Going home to an empty house—a house that has surely swelled with new sounds, new smells, the echoes of different actions—holds no appeal. He can't imagine how he could live with the cold wind boring through the valley, the sharp aching calls of a female coyote on the high ridge. Maybe if he goes back the place itself will kill him. Maybe that would be poetry enough.

He lies down on the dirty mattress and lets his failure settle onto his ribs: his failure to mourn, his failure to aim, his failure to answer Grace's signal. He curses his own distractibility. Shames himself for growing nervous when the moment was there. It's been a rare thing in his life that he pull the trigger without knowing already that the target was struck, and an impossible thing to miss once and not fire again. Had his head been a brown bottle, a half-rotted apple atop a fencepost, the hand of God Himself wouldn't have stilled a second shot.

He thinks about Sadler, the snake coursing down her arm toward her shoulder, the dark blood on her cheeks. The trembling muscles of the serpent on her skin, its rheumy black eyes and feral smell. Her acceptance of it astounding. He finds himself hoping he'll see her on his way back down the mountain so he can thank her for appearing, to let her know her kindness will ultimately have gone wasted but was a kindness all the same. That he is sorry for her lot in life, but that it's not so different, and probably not any worse, than anyone else's. The world a rotten place, everyone in it surviving on sinews and scraps.

But he has no idea where to find her, and it's probably not a good idea to wander around asking.

Sadler's mama is alive, though. She's called Catherine.

Celia's ghost trailed away from them after that night, though Anthony would come home drunk from time to time with her name sizzling on his tongue. Of course he knew it was his own family who'd warned Celia away, and of course he'd made them pay for the transgression: he left heat under pans when he finished cooking so they would wake to smoke burning in their lungs; he refused to bathe and, sometimes, to wear clothes; sometimes he sat at the dinner table, having given no advance notice of the pain he was in, and wept so loudly they couldn't hear themselves talking.

Tim told Grace to stay away for a while. Just long enough that he could find his own place. They were six months removed from the jungle by then and everything was chaos.

On a good day, which meant a day that Anthony hadn't gone to the yard to rage at the sky, a day when nobody had been forced to hear him keening while he mushed his sopping face and his fat lips against the bathroom floor, Tim took his brother up to Fort Philip and they sat together, taking turns at a bottle of whiskey. Tim trying his best to keep a pace with Anthony—the less for his brother to drink, the better—but finding it impossible. Above them, a pair of turkey vultures weaved an orbit around their heads.

You're trying to kill Mama, Tim said.

His brother's legs hung from the berm like a boy's. His filthy shoes and mismatched socks. Yeah, well, Anthony said. Everybody dies.

Not at the hands of their own son.

Anthony snorted. Happens more than you think.

Well.

Me ask you something, Anthony said. And tell me the truth, you lying motherfucker.

Okay. Shoot.

Was she too good for me? She acted like she was too good for me.

I can't say I ever saw her act like it, but yeah, she was too good for you.

She did at the end. She acted like it.

She acted like you were the best thing since sliced fucking bread. It's not her fault you're too stupid to see a good thing when you come across it.

Anthony sat picking at a scab on his knee. For a minute the *tic-tic-tic* of it the only sound in the entire world.

She loved you guys, he said.

We loved her, too.

His brother laughed and twisted his lips. So how come y'all did that to us? How come y'all split us up?

Tim thought about it for a minute and said, Because you were cheating on her.

Anthony made a chucking sound with his chest and leaned to spit over the ledge. Time was I'da killed you for saying that. He rearranged himself into an awkward pile, leaned against the damp planks behind him. I ain't fucked nobody else since her and me got together, and you should damn well know that.

Come on now, Ant. You been fucking yourself ever since you got back.

Punkin

Punkin Steeple came to life in the cellar of his family's tilted house, which sat on the edge of a limestone ridge and clung to the earth with timber fingertips. There were already six children in the fold, so his mother—Claire, a slight, lively woman—went to the cellar to get away from them, to endure what was to be her eleventh labor (four of the clan had died of various cause before their first birthdays, a common outcome in those days) in relative peace and with a cool air on her belly. She reclined on a pyramid of loose sweet potatoes and closed her eyes and listened to the clamor of her brood as they stomped and rumbled and shouted and fought above her: how she loved them, her people. She and her good husband Jacob and a half dozen terrors in a too-small house: she wouldn't have traded a minute for any amount of money, not for any land in any better country, not for the handsomest knight on the finest horse drawing the most beautiful carriage in the world. She had love in spades and hard-worked fingers and she fell to bed exhausted at the end of every day. These were things she valued, things that mattered to her, the things she thought of as her child worked its quickening way through her body.

When the moment was nigh, Jacob hurried to the cellar and crouched before his wife and opened his hands like a shortstop fielding a bumbling ground ball. Claire leaning back with her eyes closed, breathing the fine dust of their summer harvest, gripping a sweet potato in each palm, that she might channel the pain into something other than herself: they'd done this before.

The first thing to appear was a shock of orange hair. When it breached, Jacob smiled and looked to his wife and whispered, It's a ginger. The baby's head pressed forth and its skin, too, appeared orange in color, and when the beautiful little boy came full into the world, Jacob wrapped him in a cotton cloth and handed him to Claire, who needed but once to look at him before whispering, Oh, hello, Punkin.

❦ ❦ ❦

Grace had always loved that Claire Steeple found joy in what others might have considered hard living: scarce food, a tight home, the difficult work of keeping seven children fed and clothed and relatively clean, of keeping herself and her good husband Jacob from murdering each other.

It reminds me of us, she'd said. Well. Parts of it, anyway.

❦ ❦ ❦

Within a few years Punkin carried more weight than his oldest brother and was nearly as tall as Jacob himself. He operated with a kind of untameable energy, so much so that his parents joked there was a critter inside him itching to bust out, and he entertained the family by performing feats of ridiculous strength: he'd put his sisters Eloise and Justine in the palms of his outstretched hands and they'd cross their legs and close their eyes and Punkin would walk around singing what he imagined to be gypsy songs. He once bet his brothers that he could lift the entire house up by its cornerpiece, and had proceeded to do so, gently as you please. Once, their draft horse, Lovie, got his hooves lodged in a pot of quicksand past the potato field and Jacob hitched Punkin to the beast with hooks and a hawser and slapped him on the rear end and the boy damn near pulled the horse over the side of the ridge.

The consequences of this untamed clout, though, were not always so amusing. Punkin nearly decapitated a boy at school for pulling Eloise's pigtails; he'd simply lifted the child by the sides of his face, swung him around, and dispatched him over a fence that separated the playground from the road. No more difficult than chucking an unwanted stone from the garden. He removed well covers with a flick of the wrist, drained ponds with great strokes of a cupped hand so the children could look for tadpoles, and broke into the junkyard on weekends to make obscure, jagged sculptures with the engine blocks of busted automobiles—an offense for which he suffered the frequent bite of a vicious, rawboned mutt named Bastard. He was strong enough to lift he house from its foundation, but spent much of his time turned backward in the corner of the dining room, thinking, as Claire had told him to, about what he'd done.

It was clear enough to Claire and Jacob that, like many children born with extraordinary gifts, Punkin was bored by his strength and constantly searching for new challenges, new tests of his ability. He was a good kid at heart. A great kid, even, but he'd been given this powerful animal and no leathers with which to harness it. Jacob and Claire were at a loss for how to guide him. He was not smart, would never have been a philosopher or a pediatrician, but Punkin was immense help around the farm and a fine protector to his siblings. He made his way into adolescence with the same general sense that most kids his age held: that life was not as exciting as it once had been, that adults were not totally to be trusted, that patterns and repetition and sameness screwed the joy from days, that oversleeping and acting the insufferable lout were the safest ways to proceed.

And then, war.

Why are you telling me this? Tim said. Why go on and on about things that never happened?

Did you ever see a flock of birds leaving out from a tree full of leaves? Grace said.

I probably have.

And did you know they were there before they flew away?

Probably not.

Well, Grace said, and put her hand on his. The tree is the tall tale, and the birds are the truth.

In 1940 the oldest Steeple boys—Dickie, Artie, Matty, and Boyd—enlisted in the army, hopeful that if the States were dragged into the war they'd be sent to Europe together. Punkin, two feet taller than any of them and two years younger than the youngest, tagged along, sat outside the dusty little office tapping his shoes while his brothers did their duty. When they came out, they were riled and chatty, and on the way home they gabbed excitedly about the creative ways they would murder Adolf Hitler, should the opportunity ever present itself.

I'm gonna dig his heart out with my fingernails, Artie said.

I'll jam my rifle up his asshole and pull the trigger when it gets to his belly, Boyd said.

Dickie said, I'd like to punch him in the teeth and put my boot on his neck when he's down. I wanna see his eyes pop out of his head. I wanna see some dogs chew his nose off while he's still breathing.

Dickie always the most aggressive one. His brothers laughed and laughed.

And Punkin laughed along with them, skipped his awkward, orangey bulk down the street the same way they did, whistled at the girls with their same manufactured confidence. They were going to war, goddammit! They were off to serve their country, to protect those girls' right to wear their short dresses, to be beautiful and sexy and free, and when they came home, they'd take those same girls into their rooms and make babies with them and treat them like the fine country animals they were.

The truth was, though, that talk of hearts and eyeballs and assholes, talk of death and freedom and sex with beautiful girls, made Punkin sick to his stomach. He wanted to stay as far away from Adolf Hitler as possible. Newspaper photographs of the stunted dictator, with his severe haircut and his pervert's mustache, frightened him terribly. Also, he wouldn't know what to do with a woman if he caught one, and she certainly wouldn't know what to do with him. To top it off, he absolutely did not want to die.

That night, Claire found her baby boy in the attic, scrunched into an impossibly small corner, weeping.

I don't want to go, he said.

You don't have to, she said. You're too young.

What if it takes so long that I'm not too young anymore?

Oh, baby, Claire said, and wrapped her slender arms around as much of his shoulders as she could. We'll just cross that bridge when we come to it.

❧ ❧ ❧

Let me guess, Tim said. They came to it.

Well, Grace said. Sorta.

❧ ❧ ❧

On his eighteenth birthday Punkin Steeple ran away. Claire and Jacob had gone to the room he'd once shared with his brothers, carrying a small cake and a single present—a harmonica, which Punkin had always wanted—wrapped in newsprint, but they'd found the room empty. The four older boys long gone, dispersed like seeds to the far edges of their known universe: Arty in Hawaii, Dickie in Puerto Rico, Boyd in Alaska, Matty in Kansas. Punkin had pushed all five beds together to make a space almost big enough that he could stretch out in it. That morning, though, his gigantic pallet was neatly tucked and unslept-in.

When he disappeared, Punkin had been nearly ten feet tall and weighed as much as a hack pony. His bright orange hair had only gotten more so, though the pigment of his skin had faded some; in a line with his brothers he'd still have stuck out like a massive carrot among washed parsnips. He was visible from the front porch to town, and his booming voice could be heard from a mile away above a thunderstorm. But when Claire and Jacob went out that morning to search for him, they found only footprints to the main road, and once they hit pavement there was no way to guess which way their baby boy had turned.

They spent the night and the following day and the day after that wandering the lee hills and the sun-drenched cowpastures, calling the name of their giant offspring. They couldn't have known that Punkin was already deep in a mountainside, having remembered an abandoned mine his brother Arty had once told him about and in which he'd sometimes dreamed of living, that he'd brought along a sack of sweet potatoes and a bag of handmade candles, that he'd sealed himself inside with a massive hunk of concrete that had once been the base of the tipple, and that they'd not see him again for another fifteen years.

⁂

What would he have eaten, Tim said. Fifteen years is a long time to go hungry.

What difference does it make what he ate, Grace said.

And why didn't he just move the stone? He put it there in the first place. Why not move it back?

I'm getting to that.

⁂

A lot changed in those fifteen years. Boyd and Dickie Steeple both dead—Boyd had been playing cards in a house in Saint Lo when a mortar came through the roof, and Dickie contracted pneumonia and died at the rear of the Bulge. Matty and Arty had come home and pooled their money, and the money of several other men, to open Steeple Bros. Ford, an enterprise that made them both wealthy, rich enough to demolish their parents' rickety upright shoebox and put a spanking-new brick rancher in its place, wealthy enough to move into town and forget they ever knew how it felt to be busted. Eloise and Justine, the two little girls, had both married soldiers home from the Pacific; Eloise was in Charleston now, working at her husband's cigarette counter, while Justine spent her days filing legal documents in Cincinnati.

Eisenhower had won the war, and then the White House, as a sort of thank-you.

In 1948, a young real estate developer bought the old Winchester Coal and Coke: the land, the tipple, the acreage undercut by the sprawling mine. He used explosives to demolish the buildings and had it all hauled away in dump trucks. For a year the land rumbled and shifted. Coal dust rained onto Punkin's head while he slept. He was certain the war had finally reached him, that Hitler had arrived in the yard of his ancestral home, but he was far too afraid to go and see for himself. Eventually the clamor stopped (a mall now stretched for a quarter-mile above his head, its five thousand parking spaces, its eateries, its women's clothiers, its magazine stand and hat shop and candy store; when they'd finally decided it was time to hold a memorial for Punkin, Claire bought her mourning dress there during the opening-day extravaganza of Harold's Finery, unaware that her boy was already underground, that he was no more than seventy-five feet away from her, separated by nothing but concrete and dirt and timber frame and the rank, heavy air of the mine), and Punkin put his hands on the enormous block and tried to shove it away but found the strength he once had was gone. His arms like pick-up sticks, spaghetti noodles.

While he stood there puzzling, the ground began again to shake, and with a great screeching racket his concrete door was lifted from its spot by the snake-tongued prongs of a forklift, and for the first time in over a decade light shone in on the mine, along the dirt walls and down the endless shaft and all across the skin of the creature that used to be Punkin Steeple.

Creature? Tim said.

He's been fifteen years underground, love. He can't possibly be the same as he used to be.

But he's not even human anymore?

The forklift driver told police, reporters, and friends at the local greasy spoon—anyone who would listen, really—of the slender white animal he'd seen dart from the mineshaft that morning: its milky, almost translucent skin; its bulging black eyeballs big around as hockey pucks. It was naked and shivery and had raised its jagged hands in a feeble attempt to defend itself from the sunlight. The driver had locked eyes with it for a second before it took off, running a crooked course across the parking lot and over the hillside and into the stream on the far end of the property, looking not so much human as amphibian, not so much scared as lost on the surface of the sun.

A legend quickly arose in the hollers and gaps, in pre-service church pews and on the wind that blew over the creeks: an animal never before seen by men of any land now wandered the woods of Lancaster County. A beast that stole chickens from coops and bit off their heads and left their carcasses behind to soak in pools of blood. Dogs that disappeared from yards, their empty chains stretched into the dust. A woman whose daughter ran off with her boyfriend called the police and told them she'd seen a little white animal slithering out of her daughter's window that very same night. The girl came home, blushing and adjusting her skirt and smelling of cigarettes, while a sheriff's deputy spoke to her mother on the front lawn. His leather holster conspicuously unbuttoned, his hand laid on the grip and ready to draw.

Soon enough, Punkin Steeple earned himself a new name: The Hill Country Haint.

Everyone's heard of The Hill Country Haint, Tim said.

I'm trying to tell you, Grace said. These things really do happen.

Late one fall Claire and Jacob sat on the porch of their lovely brick house, watching the leaves change color. They had learned to live with Punkin as nothing more than memory, learned to cherish the small things he'd once loved; each in their own way remembered the sound of his laugh, the movement of air when he crossed through a room. They taught themselves to hope he was somewhere more comfortable for someone as big as he was—among the tall trees, maybe, high up in the mountains. They imagined him crossing ridges with no more effort than it took others to mount a flight of stairs. They imagined him swimming in lakes, his head just visible, just there, way out in the middle, alongside the wind-whipped peaks of crystal water.

Claire left Jacob alone and went inside to put the kettle on, and while she was gone, Jacob thought he saw movement in the treeline a couple hundred yards from the house. The skittering of leaves, rapid refractions of the dim evening light. He sat forward in his chair and squinted.

What is it? Claire said, standing at the screen door and looking out into the bush.

Don't know, Jacob said. Deer, maybe.

Look there, Claire said, startled, and sure enough, the little white thing whisked out of the forest then and charged toward the house, its head down like a dog on a scent, the little bulb of a tail erect and swishing.

Jesus Christ, Jacob said, and ran to get his shotgun. He shouldered the weapon and pushed the door open with the barrel and when he pulled the hammer, the animal stopped in its tracks and stood on hind legs no longer than bowling pins, sniffing the air, eyeing the dangerous folks on the porch, stuck in the impossible ether between past and future. It glanced toward the woods, and that's when they heard the voices pitched back in the trees. After a few seconds, the flicker of lanterns. Not long until their front field was full of men, twenty or more, each with a light on his belt and a weapon at his chest. The animal stuck helplessly between. Claire would later claim she could see Punkin's heart beating through the pale jelly of its skin.

It's him, one of the men shouted, it's the Haint, and like a Civil War regiment they all shouldered their weapons and Punkin turned back to his mother and for the tiniest fraction of a moment she saw her baby boy in those horrible black eyes before the first shot was fired, and then the rest of the men fired too and the animal's tiny, brittle body was torn apart in a misty cloud of blood, bullets slicing through him, exploding in the dirt around him, his innards churning into the buggy evening air and bits of him peeling off and scattering across the earth until the gunfire was over and the entire valley shouted the rapport and tasted of the smoky remainders of his killing.

We got the Haint, one of the breathless men shouted, and the rest followed in a reverie of hoots and hollers, the great belly-deep laughter of relief.

I think it's really him, Jacob whispered to his wife. He lowered the hot barrels of his shotgun. Good riddance, you son of a bitch.

Knowing

IN THE MIDDLE OF THE NIGHT he opens his eyes and he's aware that Sadler is beside him on the mattress. Her steady breathing and her arm thrown over his chest. Apart from the small rising and falling arc of her, she is still. He has a fierce urge to adjust himself, to roll onto his side, but he doesn't want to wake her, so he holds his spot, fights against his own personal gravity for the sake of her restfulness.

The night is long and warm and the crown of Sadler's head still bears the odor of fresh blood. He lies until the sun comes up, thinking of ways to move her and rejecting them, thinking of how he might slip out from beneath her without causing her to stir, but doing no such thing.

Do you remember the moment you knew I was yours? Grace asked him one morning. They were on the porch in the cut, still totally new to everything: to the day, to the farm, to their shared life and their bound livelihoods. Grace with a book spread across her lap, Tim oiling his shotgun, cleaning its hinge, wiping its barrel.

He said, I thought the days of a man owning a woman were over.

I don't mean *owning*, Grace said. I just mean knowing I wasn't going to go anywhere.

You think somebody can know that for absolute certain about somebody else?

His wife looked out over the creek, the flat rock, the sun playing on the water. Well, I sure hope so, she said.

I'm not going anywhere, he said.

I know you're not.

He looked up from his work and smiled into the sun. Maybe it's the day we got married.

Too easy. It had to have been before that, or you wouldn't have married me.

Alright, then. Maybe it's the first time we spent the night together.

Grace pouted and slapped him with her book. Fucking doesn't mean anything anymore, she said. Come on now. Get serious.

He picked his rag up and sat running it over the blue-black gun barrel. Quiet for a minute, then two.

Do you remember one night we went out to my mama's house, he said. She was on an awful drunk. Called me to come rescue her.

Now you're getting somewhere, Grace said, and leaned her head against the house and let him tell it.

He and Maksik and Sizemore sat together at a decimated table, everyone else having left out for the dance floor, the liquor in their systems propelling them to do something they had no business doing. The music thumping, the noise of joy echoing against the walls of the Victory VFW. Somewhere between the ceremony and the reception, Sizemore had fallen in love with one of Grace's cousins, a skinny blond teenager who'd come in with her family from northern Virginia. He sat watching her dance, only half-committed to his friends, his eyes following the girl's thin legs, her stockinged feet gliding across the linoleum. Some teenaged boy, a kid Tim didn't recognize, had taken her hand and was swinging her around like a bag in the wind.

Little faggot doesn't know what he's doing, Sizemore grunted. He took a long pull from his beer and turned to Tim and Maksik. You cocksuckers seeing this? This little faggot doesn't know what he's doing.

She doesn't seem to be minding, Maksik said.

Of course she minds, Sizemore said. He's got no idea what to do with her. Look at him. Looks like he caught a fish and now he's too pussy to take it off the hook. He grunted again and shook his head.

Maksik said, What the fuck are you talking about?

You gotta take the next step, son, Sizemore shouted, but everyone's ears were too full of music and booze to hear. Take her in the mop closet and bend her over, you fucking pussy.

Tim slapped Maksik on the shoulder. Speaking of that, he said, you're a married man now, too.

Yeah, that sorta happened by accident, Maksik said. Two people that didn't know each other from Adam got all dressed up and walked into a church on the same day and now they're bound by Christ and they share a last name and they got identical checkbooks for the same empty bank account.

Sounds like a nightmare, Sizemore said. He never stopped eyeballing the blond girl.

Maksik wrapped his three fingers around the neck of his beer bottle, like a mechanical claw at the junkyard. There are some days when life and a nightmare don't look much different, he said. But most times, I'd say the idea of just being a part of something is enough to make a day worth facing.

And now you got a kid of your own, Sizemore said.

Yeah, well, Maksik said. VFW in Little Rock has a mop closet, too.

Three in the morning and his mama on the other end of the phone, blubbering so hard he could only make out every fourth or fifth word. He thought for a minute she was dying. Sounded like someone had slit her throat and she was trying to explain life to him through a mouthful of blood. Something about men and motherfuckers. Something about his brother. Something about someone being too old for a baby.

He set the receiver in its cradle and swung his legs to the floor, rubbed his eyes quietly for a minute. Goddammit, he whispered.

What is it? Grace said, stirred from sleep, cinching her face as though if she could pretend she wasn't awake long enough she wouldn't be.

Mama, he said. She's all the way gone. I gotta go calm her down.

I'm coming with you.

No, you're not. Stay here and sleep. I'll be back.

They weren't yet married, weren't yet living in the cut. The rented house on Allen Street was small and smelled of bread, its shiplap walls still raw, its plumbing still shaky. The floors screamed when someone walked across them crosswise.

Grace flipped the covers away and went naked to the foot of the bed, put on yesterday's underwear, yesterday's t-shirt.

Stop me, she said.

They drove out of town: past the A&P whose lights were already burning, the stockboys kneeling in aisles with their fingerless gloves on and their crusty morning eyes; past the house where he'd spent the first years of his life, with his mother and father and Anthony; a new family manufacturing their own problems there now, solving them in whatever ways they saw fit. Every once in a while the two young boys who lived there would be on the front lawn, riding training-wheeled bikes, picking their noses, swatting at each other with whatever weapons came to hand. Their mother, or anyway some broken woman young enough to be their mother, watching from the stoop, hands clasped and with a detached expression, as though she were dreaming about Paris.

They turned down a dirt access road and cut through a mile of timber stand, reconnected with pavement at Alum Springs Road, pulled up to his mama's house just as the pink sun was licking the trees on the mountaintop.

It's hard to say—, he said.

Stop it, she said. I know it. Let's just go get her.

❦ ❦ ❦

He wakes to eggs frying and a dull soreness in his mouth. The trailer bright, the windows wedged open with chocks of wood. The door hanging wide and a perfect day bursting in like an atom bomb.

Well, ho-lee crow, Sadler sings. She's at the kitchen counter, working a pan over a kerosene campstove. She points to a chipped ceramic pitcher he'd seen in one of the cabinets. Says, I made some coffee.

He's disoriented; Sadler is doing something that he'd not considered possible in this place: he'd come here to die, after all, to mourn and then to die, and when he'd first found the trailer, it seemed the exact right place to do it. The details all ripe for a disaster. But she's not dying. Not at all. On the contrary, she's doing the things a person might do if they *lived* here, and if they intended to *go on* living here.

He pushes himself up onto his elbows and says, I didn't hear you come in.

That's because I'm a ghost. She jiggles the pan a little and takes it off the flame, sets it on a folded towel. Don't have any plates, so this'll do. You eat, I'll eat, we'll all be happy.

He ambles over, leans on the counter for a second while his legs warm up. I looked for you after the service.

I know, I know, I'm sorry. I didn't know I would have to stay. She hands him a fork, slices an egg open in the pan with her own.

I saw you, though. I saw why you had to stay.

I know you did. She swallows and wipes a dribble of yolk from the corner of her mouth. Can we let it be what it is, or are you gonna need to talk about it?

⁂

His mama was sitting in a dry bathtub with the curtain drawn. It took some time to find her: they'd called and called and gotten no response, and Tim had found himself on the back patio, staring across the rented yard, across the rented hillside. Hoping for movement, her telltale strangled cough, the homing beacon of her cigarette cherry pulsing behind the trees. When he swung the storm door open and came back inside, he heard her crying in the bathroom.

Grace had worked herself into the tub and was tangled up in his mama's legs. The two women in their blue jeans and sneakers and t-shirts; both of them had strands of hair stuck to their cheeks with tears, looking for all the world like a mother and daughter crying over a common cause. The same faded spot on their knees. The same shuffle in their throat when he came to the door. The same look in their eyes that told him he was no longer necessary here and should wait for them outside.

❦ ❦ ❦

She pulls a half loaf of bread from her bag and they sit mopping the butter and yolk from the pan and washing the food down with water from her plastic bottle.

Probably about time to get to a doctor with that face, she says.

It's alright. It's not infected.

You're the worst camper I ever met, she says.

Tim sits working the food in his good cheek, the teeth on the good side of his mouth. I don't doubt it.

You don't even have a canteen. You hardly brought any food.

Well, he says. I know a fella can hook me up with as many canned peaches as I can eat, whenever I want.

She smiles, presses a bite of bread into her cheek. Hey, I know that guy.

❦ ❦ ❦

He'd sat on the patio an hour or two, let the air get cooler and damper on his arms before the first red-orange light rose over the woods, over Fort Philip, and he watched it cast itself into the yard and crawl, like a beggar, to his feet. Grace came out and sat on his knees, the camp chair groaning under their burden.

She's sleeping, Grace said.

I don't know what you did, he said.

Not a lot.

She riled up about Anthony?

Doesn't matter.

Or she's mad she doesn't have a grandbaby yet.

I said it doesn't matter. Take me for breakfast.

❦ ❦ ❦

He set the shotgun against the door and watched the grass waving in the wind, the rippled creekwater and its thousand tiny explosions underneath the skinny-dipping stone.

Grace with her head leaning backward, her eyes closed and a contented look on her face. That's a good way to know I'm yours, she said. I'm glad you came up with that. So much better than the first time you got laid. She screwed up her face and said, Ayuk, yuk, yuk, hey, fellas, I got some ass. Har har har.

You never did tell me what she was going on about, he said.

She picked up her book and pretended to read it, the moment over.

Grace, he said.

She was missing your daddy, Tim.

Well, he said after a minute. Funny way to show it.

Grace slapped the book back down on her legs. How would you suppose someone ought to show something like that?

He looked at her stupidly because he didn't know.

She wasn't even drunk, Grace said. Did you know that? She wasn't drunk. She was scared. She thought she was dying.

Either/Or

THAT SHE'S ACTIVELY IN THE PROCESS of saving his life seems beyond question, though the *why* of it lingers, like smoke: the why of her kindnesses, the why of her sex, the why of her religion and the reasons she's chosen to share it. When she smiles, he sees the absolute rejection of hopelessness. The mere fact of her survival in this insane countryside evidence enough of a sort of faith. He wants to ask what she sees in him worth saving, but he's afraid of finding her answer too agreeable.

Today is your last day here, she tells him. She dumps a palmful of salt into the pan and scours out the fat and crusted yolk with her fingertips.

What makes you say that?

Well, she says. Technically, you're squatting on my property. The house being mine and all. She looks up at him. That's in the will, if you need to see it.

So that's your reason? Trespassing?

She smiles. Of course not.

So what is it, then?

She slides the pan into her bag and comes over and puts her hand on the good side of his face and stands on her tiptoes and kisses him. It's because I'm coming with you, she says.

He and Maksik stood smoking outside the VFW, watching Sizemore puke in the street. The night was damp, water vapor like ghostly bloodspray wafting from streetlamp to streetlamp, and the party had disintegrated, guests gone off to their houses or back onto the highway for their drunken drives to wherever. Grace at her parents' to change out of her dress and watch TV. She'd be asleep on the couch by the time he got to her.

What the fuck is your fucking problem, Maksik said. His face twisted. He flicked his cigarette at Sizemore's feet.

Sizemore stood buckled at the waist, chucking bits of vomit from between his teeth and laughing. I'm just so godawfully alone, he said, and shook his head from side-to-side like a horse with a loose halter.

And then there he was, standing across the street, a phantom with a cigarette wedged deep between his fingers, a baseball cap pulled low to his eyes, but it was surely him: Dean Goodell. They all three noticed him at once.

Motherfucker, Sizemore whispered.

Don't forget it's a party, Kenny, Goodell said. He drew on his cigarette one last time and dropped it, ground it into the sidewalk with his toe. Congratulations, Country. My God, Grace is a one-of-a-kind beauty.

I have to go get my gun, he says.

She pushes a ball of bread into her cheek, says, Let me do it.

They walked toward the astringent neon light of a bar at the end of the block and turned in and found a table up front where Goodell could see out the window. He looked like hell and wore his twenty-five years like fifty: his face gray, his hair receding, though his muscles were still taut beneath his shirt. He'd developed the cough of a long-time smoker, a black-lunger, bad enough that he was forced sometimes to double over until it cleared. It was probably fortunate that neither he nor Sizemore had the gumption to fight; Sizemore had never failed to mention his continued hatred for Goodell. *Pussy* the word most often used, *pussy* being the word most often used by Sizemore for nearly everything, when *traitor* would have done as well, and been perhaps more to the point. *Turncoat*. *Judas*. *Benedict Arnold*.

But the fact of his sitting there, if even for a few minutes, in a wide-open watering hole in the middle of downtown Victory, West Virginia; the fact that he'd made it out of the jungle, that he'd made it at least to Bangkok, and maybe to Bali, like he'd said he would; that he'd not fired on a single human being past the day he realized he could no longer stand the weight of being a soldier and had disappeared instead through that little bear-tunnel at the far edge of camp; all of it came together to impress Tim, in the end. There had certainly been nights when Tim had lain in his little tent at the edge of some rice paddy in the deepest recesses of a war he didn't understand and thought hard about ways to slaughter Dean Goodell: just to shut him up, just to keep him from scratching at Tim's tent like a street cat begging to be let in. But the gaunt little shit that sat hunched in front of them, shoulders tight against his cheeks while outside, the West Virginia night grew blacker and cooler and more total, held some kind of value that Tim never expected he would. Surely a man who can walk calmly away from that kind of horror is of some consequence. Surely a man who notices a great moral failing and objects—though it may cost him his life, his rank, his friends, his future; though it may cost him his freedom, his manhood, the respect of his father and brothers and uncles, any woman he may have wanted to sleep with—surely that kind of a man has something inside him worth learning, a sermon heretofore misunderstood but nevertheless worth preaching.

I've wanted to kill you for years, Sizemore grunted. He leaned on Tim's shoulder for support.

Sorry, Kenny, but I can't stay, Goodell said.

Did I see you once? Tim said. A while back, me and Grace were over in Virginia, and then there you were. I thought my eyes were playing tricks on me.

Goodell lit a cigarette and pulled the ashtray closer and kept eying Sizemore. His look one of sympathy. Don't think that must have been me, no, he says. Only been one or two places since I got back, and I don't like to speak the names of either. Hell, I didn't even keep my own name. Ever since I'm home I've been calling myself Kenneth J. Sizemore.

Sizemore pulled his head up and bared his teeth.

People could always tell I was a psycho, Goodell said. I just figured being a Sizemore made me some kind of famous.

❧ ❧ ❧

She's brought a change of bandage in her backpack and he leans as still as he can against the counter while she strips the old one off and swabs at the wound with an alcohol pad. You're right, she says, it's not infected, but it may yet get there. The stitches look good, anyway.

Catherine was a steady hand, he says.

She's like that.

She stretches the new bandage across his cheek and tapes it around the edges several times over.

There's one other thing, she says.

What is it?

What to do about Jonas.

What about him?

Technically, I'm the legal guardian.

What does that mean, technically?

It means I have the same say his mama would have had if she'd been alive.

Why isn't that his daddy's job?

You know enough about his daddy to understand how that must have played out.

❧ ❧ ❧

Goodell made it to Bangkok almost entirely on foot and worked his way down the Malay Peninsula, avoiding the worst of the dense western jungle by following the coast, buying his passage south on a series of Jon boats and dugouts intended for softer water. Harrowing experiences alongside fisherman whose lives were harried enough that they'd grown accustomed to it. Men who stood at the ends of their rigs, casting, licking their sun-chapped lips, cracking jokes in a language he was hopeless to understand. Their skin deep brown like tree roots. Their teeth chipped or missing. They smoked a ceaseless supply of cigarettes and carefully squeezed the cherries into the ocean before crushing the butts flat and slipping them into their pockets. Goodell had abandoned his carbine before he walked into Bangkok—too bulky, too American—but held onto his Colt, and he would sometimes brandish it and fire wildly into the water off the side of the boat, which set the fishermen to guffawing while they tugged at the handlines of ancient nets that had belonged to their fathers and their grandfathers before that.

In Singapore he took his first shower in over a month and fell in love with a woman.

To save, or perhaps to condemn. Sadler's leaving with him carried the flavor of either, of both. They didn't know each other. The one unaware of the other's dangers. Their misgivings. Their allegiances. When the snake had twisted its way down Sadler's arm and she'd tilted her head back in some kind of strange euphoria, it occurred to him there were times they didn't even speak the same language. Hers a loose translation of the word of God, his a thoughtless but consistent rebuttal. Still, she was grown; if she was ready to pack her bag and walk down into the great wide world it wasn't for him to stop her.

To bring the brother along was different. Messier. Jonas' place in the world was harder to know, and would only grow harder; a universe of options, the sea of faces that swelled and retracted in the everyday, were not necessarily good things for someone like him. Easy enough to see a future of casting him out and guiding him back in, of hurting and comforting, of teaching and reforming.

It was foolish, but not insane, to think of a future with Sadler McIntire as adventure; impossible to think of a future with Sadler and Jonas both as anything other than family.

Elena was fleshy, dark-haired, smooth. Sexy, if you didn't look past her knees: one of her feet was clubbed, having been mangled in childhood by a water monitor's bite, which grew so infected she'd had to have three toes removed. The rest of the appendage curled in on itself like a rotten fruit. She walked with the aid of a crutch and never made a big deal out of it. Held a good job as an assistant to an office of doctors. She was constantly laughing, constantly jabbing Goodell in the ribs for his stupid Americanisms. She was a paradox: she insisted on dressing him like a proper Singaporean, but she loved Clint Eastwood and Marilyn Monroe and walked through her small, tidy apartment singing "Hound Dog," twisting her naked hips in a comely Presley tribute, the rubber tip of her crutch thrumming on the floor beside her.

Goodell dug through the bowl of stale peanuts in front of them, searching for the ones without skins, talking, talking. Sizemore asleep against the wall, and Maksik with a group of toughs at the dartboard who'd been more than happy to accept his drunken bets. But Tim sat still, quietly transfixed by Goodell's story, listened intently as though missing something and trying to recreate it; because Goodell was sitting across from him in this unlikely place, this place Tim knew well and frequented for an after-work beverage with his crew but that Goodell had never seen before and would never see again; it seemed obvious that things with his beautiful Elena had not worked out. It seemed obvious that Goodell would be driving home that night to wherever he was living, whatever shanty on whatever hillside, whatever shitty little flat above whatever laundorama, and that he'd be alone when he got there. That he'd eat a cheap meal from the freezer, tug on himself in the shower with his head down, go to sleep in a bed with no sheets and a folded pair of blue jeans for his pillow. It seemed obvious these were the things his life would have afforded him and, more than that, that these were the things he'd willingly accept from the world as his personal vision of plenty.

What brought you back? Tim said. Goodell had paused in his story, sat gazing over Tim's shoulder into the street.

My mother got cancer, Goodell said. Yeah, by the time her letter got to me in Singapore, she only had a few months to go.

Did you get to see her?

Yeah. I did. She looked like shit.

How'd you get home?

Same way anyone else would. We got on a plane and flew.

We?

Yeah, *we.* I told Elena she either had to come or I wasn't going. So she came.

Bodies

THEY AGREE TO TAKE THE DAY so she can gather necessities—her brother, some clothes, the pistol from Wiley and Catherine's. While she's there, she'll say goodbye to her mother. Their plan is to meet at the trailer at dark and walk down the mountain in the moonlight, with the goal of making it to the main road by morning. She promises to bring sandwiches and a bottle of Coke apiece.

From the yard she looks back at him, squints in the sunlight. You reckon they'll put me on a milk carton?

You're too big for that now, he says. They'll say you made your own choices.

You reckon Daddy'll follow me?

I couldn't say for certain, but I think I would if I was your daddy.

But you ain't.

Thank God for that.

You don't have much in common with my daddy.

No, and I can't say I'm sorry you feel that way.

Well, I mean, other than the obvious, she says.

Which is what?

She points at her cheek to indicate his own. We're all sinners, Peaches. Your body is the temple of the Holy Spirit, who God gave you. It doesn't belong to you. You shouldn't have done what you did.

Goodell and Elena sat in a Charlottesville hospital for the better part of two weeks, watching his mother die from the inside out. Waiting for the machines to quit their pulsing. Waiting for the nurses to slow down, for the scramble to be unnecessary. Now and then the old woman would attempt a bite of something, Jell-O or pea soup or applesauce, but most of it dribbled down her sharp jowls to settle in the folds of her neck. Now and then she summoned the strength to sit up long enough to say a few incoherent words, to smile at her son who'd come all the way from the South Pacific and whom she didn't know anymore. These things gave Goodell hope, not because they meant she would go on living, but because they were evidence that her death would not be without mercy. That she made a dignified attempt at all, that she was trying to carry on with life's necessary forces, was both heartbreaking and darkly beautiful.

The great injustice of Vietnam, Goodell said, tapping the bottom of an empty bottle on the tabletop, is not that so many of us ate shit, but that so many more of us came home knowing we weren't invincible. See, when you're nineteen, you're supposed to believe nothing can touch you. That your nuts are so big all you gotta do is slap somebody with them and they'll get back in line. That's how you take over the world. That's how you get big in business. That's how you run for Senate. And then somebody like Murphy—remember Murphy? From Connecticut somewhere, rich motherfucker—steps on a Betty and gets his dick blown off, balls and all. We all saw it. He's laying there cupping the bloody mess where his dick used to be, bleeding out in the grass. Two, three minutes to live. What are we supposed to do with something like that? How do we walk into a job interview with that shit stuck in our brains?

When his mother died, Goodell said, Elena sat praying with the body while he went to find the nurse. When they came back, his girlfriend's head was bent to the old woman's and there seemed to be two voices in the room, as if they were whispering to each other.

I never did figure out who was doing all the talking, Goodell said.

Once Celia was good and gone, once the dust of her had been broomed from their mama's floors, once her perfume had finally been coaxed out the windows and her dimple had risen from the mattress where she and Anthony had slept beside each other, Tim watched his brother follow a quick, spiraling pathway into hell: an insane amount of booze, the destructive search for grander and more impossible fistfights, a course of loose women, each scrawnier and cheaper than the last. Several times Tim got called to come get him from town lockup—a circumstance he despised, as Paul Pitts, the police chief in Victory, had known their father well and never missed an opportunity to remind everyone what a fuckup the old man had been.

One night Anthony got his ass kicked by a group of vets in a pool hall. When Tim went in to talk to Pitts at seven the next morning, his brother sat pressing a towel against his face that still sopped with bloodrun from his nose.

What's the bail? Tim said.

Pitts blinked at him a couple times and unclipped the keys from the hook under his belly. Just look at him, he said. He looks just like your daddy. He flicked his wrist and the cell popped open. Let's call it time served.

The toll Anthony took on his own body was incredible. He lost twenty pounds on a frame that only hung a hundred sixty to begin with. His hair grew long and matted. He took to wearing long-sleeve shirts when he went to their mother's so she would neither see nor worry about the parallel razor wounds that had sprung up across his arms, like so many uniform mountains on the floor of a pale and shallow sea.

The best Tim could ever do for his brother was to be there, to simply *arrive*, to be waiting at the bus station when Anthony came home from wherever his hungers had beckoned him: Virginia Beach, Durham, Erie. To keep the gas topped in the Ford so he could make it to the hellhole places where Anthony found himself abandoned, forgotten by some woman who'd promised to be there but wasn't, left by some woman who'd promised him a ride but reconsidered. To face down Chief Pitts in Victory Town Hall, watch the old fucker's brow wrinkle when he launched into a disassembly of Tim's people, smell the old fucker's breath while he choked himself with laughter.

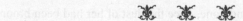

❧ ❧ ❧

He walks one last time to the creekside, sits on his rock to watch the water go by. Thinks how many hours will establish a life, how many gallons of water, how many swallows, how many breaths. The fine matter of a person's body disintegrating into the air, borne aloft on any wind at all, shed into the grass to feed the soil, sloughed away by silty creekwater on an August afternoon. And so: there are bits of Grace in this stream, bits of her in the leaves that have begun to unfold like nervous hands expecting to be slapped. A given that her memory will be with him forever, but for the first time he realizes that she will continue to be of the earth, that her body will feed its necessities, that he must no longer be nonchalant about where he places his feet, as at any moment he may be stepping on her, on the earthworm that ate of her bones, on the flower that drank of her blood.

In the afternoon he walks back out to the where the Ford sits wasting and pops the hood and looks inside, but sees nothing he knows what to do with.

⚜ ⚜ ⚜

At last call Goodell helped them pull Sizemore from the booth. Maksik knelt and let the lieutenant fall over his shoulder, carried him fireman-style back into the street where they stood for a minute in quiet disbelief: that here they were, that there they would go, that this was how life had turned out.

I have to know, Tim said, how you've managed not to get yourself arrested.

I genuinely don't know the answer to that, Goodell said. When Mom got sick, I took a chance by getting on an airplane. They didn't catch me then, so I figured they'd never catch me.

Sizemore grunted then and punched Maksik in the asscheek.

Something doing there, Maksik said, and propped the lieutenant against the building.

You're a dead man, Sizemore said. His face cool and colorless.

Come on now, Kenny, you're in no shape, Goodell said. I thought we were through. Can we let it go for a while? Maybe one day when I come through Texas, I'll stop and we can do it up right.

You dumb motherfucker, Sizemore said.

I think that's my cue to leave, Goodell said, and made to shake their hands.

I reported you dead, Sizemore said. Vaporized in a napalm strafe. Friendly fire, missed the mark. He is breathing hard. Panting. I told them it was a tragedy.

Goodell stared at Sizemore for a minute: his trembling lips, his concave chest, the pale tongue that hung between his teeth when he spat.

So what, then, Goodell said.

So they'll catch on, Sizemore said, his words slow and crooked. Sooner or later. But for now, you're a walking corpse. Nobody's laid a finger on you because nobody wants to touch a dead man.

Which was true. When Ocasio hung himself in the woods, Maksik had shimmied up the hopea and used his buck knife to slice the belts free. Ocasio's body had landed with a thud in the tall grass, his legs crumpled underneath, his eyes bulged out so far they seemed ready to burst. His pants still damp at the crotch where he'd pissed himself during the struggle.

Nobody moved. Nobody made to wrap their hands around their friend's ankles; nobody volunteered to take him under the arms. They stood in a sort of phony prayer, their arms crossed, their eyes cast toward the body. Maksik finally dropped out of the tree, called them pussies and cowards, bent down and hefted Ocasio into his arms. Carried him two hundred yards back to camp and sat there smoking with the body at his feet while he waited for a chopper to come and take it away.

He stepped into Grace's parents' house, so quiet at three in the morning that his breathing echoed down the hallway, set his shoes neatly against the wall and walked into the living room. His eyes not yet adjusted to the dark, but he could feel his wife's body in the atmosphere, the pressure change in the air when she shifted and the particulate clouds of her breathing when they moved over his skin. He went to the couch, still in his wedding clothes, and lifted the quilt. She reached around to hold it up for him and he slid in behind her, wrapped his arms around her waist to keep from falling into the floor.

You had a good time, she whispered.

No, he said. Not really.

Descent

HE WAITS FOR THEM ON THE HOOD OF THE FORD, amazed by how much dead skin can shake free from the forest in just a few short days; he pinches leaves and helicopter seeds from the wiper well and tosses them to the ground. A feeling like he'd had as a little boy—a sort of happiness, he supposes, a satisfaction that the world has been constructed for him and him alone. That there be no one else in this forest, only a wide-open space for his own thoughts; that there be no predator here, nothing of concern, nothing dangerous, just a patch of earth where the sun happens sometimes to shine and the rain happens sometimes to fall.

He knows, of course, that it's untrue, that there are now and will always be malign elements in these woods, as there are everywhere. Copperheads, black bears, destroying angels. Whoever had owned the voices that night, the night his brother had gone on sleeping and Tim had lain awake with arms pulled inside his t-shirt, awaiting his own slaughter. He and everyone he knows has heard tell of flash floods sweeping through hollers, babies swept from mothers' arms, men decapitated by tumbling appliances full of mud. Stories of wild-eyed hatchet men, fires that rolled over the landscape like milk across a table. A hundred ways to die anywhere, and the forest no exception.

Picking at this thoughts, he hears soft voices on the hillside, jumps down, and straps his father's duffel across his chest.

❦ ❦ ❦

And then, one day, nothing. A day into a week, a week into a month. Tim and Grace well settled into the cut by then: pulling in pay, scrambling eggs from their own chickens, following the common pattern in pursuit of a break in it, which would itself become part of the pattern. He heard nothing from Anthony, bad or good, received no calls from the chief, heard of no woman his brother had somehow managed to fuck over or be fucked over by. Their mama didn't call with any new emergency, but did offer that Anthony had been going somewhere on Sunday mornings, though he wouldn't say where, and somewhere else on weekdays that she assumed was a sort of job but didn't ask about, too afraid to break a streak of luck. Every Friday he came home with an armload of groceries and once in a while he even cooked something. Sometimes she'd watch him sink silently to the ground and do thirty or forty push-ups. Fifty sit-ups. As if a voice in his head had told him when to do them, and where. They watched the news together, but Anthony never said anything. He watched troops coming home, footage of their skinny-legged girlfriends running in for an embrace, their coquettish skirt-hems sliding unchecked up the fleshy cups of their backsides. For other people: kisses, handshakes, cigars exchanged in quick motions. Anthony had no comment on any of it, and when the programs ended, he'd go outside and smoke a couple of cigarettes and come back in and go to bed.

He'd been getting up at four in the morning. He told their mama he was writing a book, but there was no way he'd tell her what it was about and she was not, under any circumstance, to ask.

❦ ❦ ❦

A woman and a man come down from the hill, but not the two he's expecting.

Timothy, my friend, McIntire says. Tim can barely make him out in the dusklight.

We heard you was having car trouble, Mama says from somewhere in the darkness. I can fix that, you know. *Hocus pocus! Alakazam!* She cackles wildly.

I was just on my way out, Tim says.

We heard that, too, McIntire says. He's come close enough now that Tim can see him, the sharp features of his face, the pale reflection of the moon in his plastic glasses. Why we're here, in fact. Thought we might try and talk you out of it.

I appreciate that, Pastor.

But you won't be persuaded, Mama says.

I'm not real sure how persuadable I am, Tim says.

Above them on the road, the shuffle of lazy footsteps. A heavy, whumping breathing. Wiley.

I'd say plenty persuadable, McIntire says.

Tim wraps his hands around the strap of his duffel. He doesn't know what the fight will be, but he's pretty sure there's going to be one.

Did I tell you I went to war, too, Timothy? McIntire says. That's true. I did. Infantryman in the First Marines. Korea, 1951.

I had an idea about it, Tim says.

How's that?

You got the glasses for it. And the haircut.

McIntire chuckles and rubs his hand absentmindedly over his head. I guess old habits die hard, he says. He takes a step forward and Tim can smell his day-long breath, his cheap aftershave like old booze. He can hear the air whistling softly through McIntire's nose when he inhales.

Do you wanna know how I knew you were a soldier? McIntire whispers.

I dunno, Tim says.

Oh, come on, now. You guessed *me* easy enough.

Tim looks into the preacher's eyes. I'd say it was probably the gun.

McIntire turns to Mama and Wiley and laughs and the sound of it explodes into the night air. Says, He thinks it takes a gun to know a soldier! Good God almighty, boy!

Tim stands defiant. Well. Let's have it, then.

The preacher steps back in and puts his hands on Tim's shoulders. His grip is hard and painful. I used to get up in the morning and look in the mirror and see something that terrified me greatly, he says. Every day I'd hope I was looking at something unique, but I wasn't. No, no, I've seen it before, many times, and in fact I see it on you. It's a *haunting*, Timothy, you know that? A ghost under your skin. I can see your face and also the face of the man that lives inside you. A desperate, dangerous young man. He looks a lot like you, but your own mother would have a hard time in recognizing him. He's capable of anything. Any violence. And he doesn't. Ever. Go. Away.

Tim listens quietly and can't help but remember a story Grace once told him about The Hill Country Haint. *Good riddance, you son of a bitch.*

The difference between you and me, McIntire says, it that I was standing in the right place when that fellow inside of me decided to bust out.

Not long before Grace died, Maksik called from Ohio to tell him Goodell had been caught and was probably, that very moment, headed to Leavenworth on the fastest train possible.

The dumb son of a bitch was living at home with his mama, Maksik said. Didn't try to hide or nothing.

His mama's dead, Tim said.

I know that's what he said, but she sure isn't. She's how I come to know all this.

A group of MPs had taken Goodell into custody at the secondhand furniture store where he was working. They'd neglected to inform his mother, either beforehand or after, of their plans. When her son didn't come home for dinner, she called the store, which is how she knew he'd been captured, but they couldn't tell her why. So she phoned everyone she could think of, and when nobody knew anything, she went through his room and started calling numbers he'd written down in random places—notebooks, napkins, receipts for fast-food dinners.

Eventually, she gets ahold of me, Maksik said. My wife answers, and I can hear from across the room some hysterical woman on the other end blubbering and crying, and Kim just hands the phone to me, all natural, like of course this must be *my* problem. He chuckled, as though any of it were funny.

Jesus Christ, Tim said. What about Elena?

Hey, Maksik said, there's the kicker—there was *no Elena.*

What?

Squirrelly little bastard made the whole thing up, you believe that? He really did run away, we all know that, and maybe he actually made it to Bali or Singapore or wherever the fuck, but he never had no girl named Elena. Far as I can tell, this Elena broad never even existed.

One day he and his brother came home from school to find a pile of dusty equipment at the end of the driveway. An old yoke and plow assembly, a stack of barn windows, some pails and brushes, a dented welder's mask, a pair of leather gloves. They took turns wearing the mask and slapping each other across the face. Tim laughing, though his brother's strikes were hard enough to twist the plate sideways on his head. Inside a corn seed bag they found a block and tackle and a length of rope and Anthony said, Lookit here. Fort Philip just got itself an elevator.

They devoted the entire weekend to building it. They extended a beam from the highest point of the structure: high enough that if one had walked it, like a plank, and tumbled from the end, he would fall twenty feet before he hit dirt, and then he'd likely tumble another hundred into the skinny creek that slunk along at the foot of the hill. They built a cantilever and a brace arm for support and made the lift from birch limbs lashed together. The block and tackle secured at the top with a rusted eye screw.

Alright, then, Anthony said, wrapping the rope around his arm and wrist. Give it a shot.

It was Sunday evening. Tim's arms sore from so much hauling, hanging, testing, twisting. The sun gone pink across the valley. Their mother overdue in shouting for dinner.

I'm not going first, Tim said. It's *your* idea. You get on the goddamned thing.

Alright then, Anthony said again, making a show of letting loose the ropes, rolling his sleeves into tight pinches at his elbows, checking and double-checking the worth of the knots that held the platform. He stood on the birch and shifted his weight from side-to-side like a man about to be hanged and looked sideways at his brother. Pull it, dickhead.

Tim hung up with Maksik still laughing on the other end of the line. He'd never realized how much respect he'd had for Dean Goodell until, in a single minute, within the span of a stupid telephone call from a crazy man in Ohio, he lost every last drop of it.

The long arm at the top of Fort Philip groaned and shuddered with Anthony's weight, but it held. Tim manning the hawser on the ground, his brother rising, rising, reaching to touch the soft green skin of leaves on his way past, looking down at Tim and smiling. Up he went, past the ramparts, past the wall that held the photograph of their father, past the original lookout tower. The sad groan of the block and tackle above his head. He came level with the platform they'd built especially for this purpose and stepped away from the elevator and onto the topmost corner of the structure, a mishmash of nails and screws and secondhand planks. Stood on the edge and hocked a lugey and shot it toward Tim, who had to sidestep to keep from getting hit in the face.

You should have taken the chance when you had it, Anthony called. He looked around him: the view, the trees, nothing but distance. Places he could run to if he'd ever had the gumption. Wish I had my rifle, he said. I could hit damn near anything from up here.

You can't hit anything from anywhere, Tim said.

Anthony spat again and it came even closer this time. I could hit you, at least, he said, and that's all that really matters.

Decisions

IT IS PAST NINE when their little group shuffles onto Wiley's front yard. His cozy house quiet and resting: light from a single room and no sign of the children, who may already be sleeping. The air cool. The wind gentle. The distant shotgun-racking sound of katydids in the trees.

McIntire pats Tim on the shoulder. We're human, Timothy, he says. We make decisions with the evidence we have available. Remember that before we go inside, because you're about to have to do it again.

Okay.

The entryway is dark. To his left, the room he'd stayed in after his fall from the fire tower. They turn through the kitchen and toward the orange glow of candlelight. Mama with her fingers on the small of Tim's back, either to show the way or to support herself in walking.

In the dimness of the sitting room two armchairs have been pulled to face each other. Catherine comfortable in one, her feet drawn under herself and a mug of tea steeping on the side table. In the other, Sadler: smiling, but maybe from nerves; when she looks at Tim he understands instantly that something is vastly different now than it had been before.

Hi, she says.

Hi.

Mama, McIntire says. Go ahead and show him, please.

There were times he thought about Goodell and the moment he entered that hole in the thicket, his first steps toward a lifetime of running, the weight of everything he'd need for survival strapped against his body. How much sweat must have been pouring into his eyes, how sore his legs must have been. Had he been freezing, or was there adrenaline enough to warm him?

And then, the moment he emerged: the night pitch-black and humid, the dry warning calls of jungle beasts, the river rushing by him, lapping at his boots with its hungry tongue. No shelter to duck into, no softly humming radio, no men chatting quietly while they smoked cigarettes outside their tentflaps. Had the planning of it begun then to break down? The sense of direction? Had the map, memorized in daylight, started to blur and disintegrate in his mind? Tim wondered if Goodell had ever thought, even briefly, of turning back.

Mama stands behind Sadler's chair and holds her hands open above the girl's head while Catherine stretches to blow out the candle. For a minute nothing happens. Tim turns to his right and left to the men beside him. He can hear their breathing, feel the skin of their arms against his own, but cannot see them. Then it begins.

And Anthony, who dealt with demons by conjuring more demons. As though his insides were a great battleground, and let the worthiest beast win: let the liquor drown the memories, let the powder dry the booze. Let the great wolf eat of the body and the mind, and thereby sate his hunger for the soul.

It's hard at first to notice the change, but the longer Mama stands with her fingers outstretched the brighter Sadler begins to glow. Her skin like a paper bag with a moon inside. She sits still and quiet, and when she smiles, her mouth opens a crack and some of the light falls out.

Their father shot himself in the head when they were only boys. Naked and wet in the bathroom, as though something unexpected just overtook him, interrupting an otherwise normal day; as though someone had pushed their finger against just the right part of his skull with just the right amount of pressure and leaned into him and whispered, *Now.*

What is this, Tim says. Sadler's shine bright enough that he can see their faces.

A beginning, Mama says.

Sadler looks at him, her eyes seeping light, the crack of her mouth, the phosphorescent tips of her hair. Tim, she says.

This is your choice, Timothy, McIntire says, loudly, to drown her out. This is the knowledge you have available to you.

Tim, Sadler says again. They're saying I'm pregnant.

Their mama had found the passion to pack their lives up and move them to the woods but lost it shortly thereafter—among the trees and the sound and the interminable boredom of watching her normal boys become typical men. And now she would live out her days there, smashing her frustration into the ashtray, harboring fantasies of her family's eventual reunion. Watching Anthony flail like a man hung by his neck. Listening for the ghost of their father, whom she sometimes heard shuffling along out on the road, calling out for her, calling out for his boys.

He can't breathe.

There is no way for them to know this. No way for them to know what has passed between himself and the girl, insufficient time to understand its consequences even if they did. Not doctors. Not midwives. They're bush magicians, purveyors of snake oil and coincidence, casting some sort of bluff.

He sucks in a lungful of heavy air and says, Bullshit.

Catherine looks at Sadler, still glowing, beautiful. Sweet girl, she says. Look what you've done.

Celia had decided to love his brother and to love him hard. Took the risk of joining their ranks, folding herself into their crazed number, stepped barefooted into their lives and offered them a type of joy they couldn't recognize. Leaned into Anthony in the back room and held his sweaty head in her lap while he suffered the jungle over and over. But kind souls will exit a nightmare: it simply isn't where they belong; it isn't where they'll be of the most use. Nobody was surprised when she slipped her sandals back on and took her Pyrex up in her hands and danced out their mama's back door the one last time. Tim had wished her well, and hoped the short trauma of being one of them for a while wouldn't hold her back from any dreams she may still have had.

His decision, initially, is to turn and run. He takes a step backward, half-expecting the men to hold him, to grab at his arms or clothes, but they don't. Sadler stands, soft light seeping through her shirt, opens her mouth to say something but keeps it to herself. Mama behind her with her hands on the girl's arms.

If you're going, Catherine says, look in the kitchen drawer beside the door on your way out.

And so he does: he hurries from the room and into the kitchen, opens the drawer and sees, amongst a mess of keys and coins and household sundry, his father's 1911. He checks the magazine, snaps a round into the chamber, and tucks the weapon into his belt. When he cracks the door, the sound outside is deafening, as if all the creatures within the deep woods have opened their mouths at once and collected themselves into a scream. A short silence, and then screaming again, as though they'd merely paused to catch their breath.

❦ ❦ ❦

Maksik cleared the jungle through voodoo and black magic. Totems hanging from his belt, a cast of spells from his idiot mouth whenever he saw fit to speak. He'd made it through by being both the dumbest and the bravest among them, by doing the things the rest of them were unwilling and unable to do; he had earned the respect of the other men, and also that of the spirit world: all the ghosts that wandered through that thick and horrendous jungle must have held him in extremely high regard, for they mostly left him alone—largely, Tim thought, because Maksik had managed to prove himself their equal.

❦ ❦ ❦

The forest is cold and pitch-black and he stumbles into it headlong, casting through trees with his arms flailing like a man treading water in a bottomless lake. Behind him the voices of McIntire and Wiley and Mama, calmer than the circumstances probably demand, for he is desperate and knows it, either at the beginning or the end of what feels very much like a long and catastrophic emergency.

❦ ❦ ❦

And Grace, whose body decided it had had enough of this world. Enough of this sunshine, enough of this argument, enough of this constant debate between her head and her lungs about how much air she needed. Enough food. Enough swimming. Enough of everything. Certainly she'd swallowed more of the world at a gulp than Tim could have done in a lifetime; still, she must have convinced herself that not only had she taken all she wanted but that she'd given all she could: that she would be leaving the world a finer place, that her parents had known some kind of joy, that Tim had been set on a straight course and would find his way out eventually, if he just kept picking up his feet and putting them down in front of himself. Had she thought any different, she would have just stuck around a while longer.

Several hundred yards from the house, his toe catches the lip of a stone and he crashes face-first into the deepening forest castoff. His hands sunken into the detritus like a child playing at the beach, his mouth gritty with soil. The handle of the 1911 pushing against his belly. He lies there for a while, spitting, his orientation off. He lifts his head and scans the ground and realizes he doesn't know the direction he's running or where he'll end up when he gets there. As likely that he falls from a cliff and gets swallowed up in the great gaping maw of a whale as anything else.

What had Sadler done? There was so little of her that he understood, so little of her past. He both knew her and didn't at all. Her intrusion into his life mere happenstance; the simple choice, made in haste by a hungry man and largely through lack of option, of a place to eat. And then, the accident of sitting next to her brother. The accident of driving up the hillside where they lived, the accident of a busted engine. The accident of bathing in the same creek she bathed in. Of sleeping on the same mattress. All of it accidental: that their skin had ever touched, that he'd found himself inside her, that it had been her face his mind had wandered to when he'd pressed the gun against the roof of his mouth. After so many thousands of decisions that made up an entire life, funny to know that it all came down to chance.

He hears the rattle before he sees the animal. A tension against his hip, a vibration, a sort of earthly warmth that he can feel through the fabric of his jeans. The sound like water pouring steady into a tin bucket. He turns slowly, his arms still stretched outward, and sees the night air shivering around the snake's tail. He can't move and doesn't want to.

Timber rattler, someone whispers.

What? Tim says into nothing.

It's a timber rattler. Big fat one.

He recognizes Jonas' voice.

What do I do?

You're in a bad spot, Jonas whispers. He's somewhere ahead of Tim, crouched in the trees.

What do I do?

Pretend you're dead. Stay still and maybe he'll leave you be.

And for a minute that's what Tim does. He tries not to breathe, afraid that lifting his spine will be seen as aggression. He leaves his hands flat against the ground and wills himself not to blink. But then he hears something, in a wind through the leaves, maybe, the slow shifting of soil beneath his head: his brother's voice saying, *Grab him.*

When he moves, the rattler moves with him, its head jolting forward, the wet mouth open wide; Tim's hand flicking quickly to his hip and latching onto the animal's thick body. Its fangs sink into the meat of his thumb, the hard jolt of electricity when the venom enters his bloodstream. He opens his mouth to yell, but no sound comes out. He hangs onto the snake for dear life, though the animal is struggling hard to wrench itself loose.

Jonas sneaks up beside him and watches this moment of violence. Watches Tim involuntarily drop the snake, and watches it fake another strike before sliding away through the leaves. He lifts Tim's hand, which has already swelled some.

Hell, he says. You'll be alright.

Insistence

WHEN IT WAS OVER, most of them sat on the warm ground and drank water and ate candy bars from their packs, wiping their forehead sweat onto their sleeves and lighting cigarettes off the cherry of the guy beside them. They watched the earth around them smoldering, faces neither satisfied nor unsatisfied: their five-day beards, their jaws working at sticks of Juicy Fruit. They swatted at the black flies in their hair and laughed and leaned back dramatically when something popped in one of the burning huts.

Tim sat a few hundred yards away, hunched over the black body of the Vietnamese boy that Goodell had roasted after he lit out from his doorway. Tim pegged the kid at maybe eleven or twelve, and realized the two of them were close enough in age that Tim could remember what it had felt like to be him: had this kid gone fishing that morning with his father? Had he made fun of his mother's cooking the night before, and had she beaten him for it? Was there some skinny, dark-haired, coal-eyed local girl who took over his brain when he lay down at night? The kid lay on his belly with his dead mouth open and blades of grass against his lips. His shirt had burned away and through layers of skin and sinew Tim could see pieces of his spine, the surrounding muscle still spasming, working against the bone to make sure he would always stand straight.

He borrowed an E-tool from somebody and walked back to where the boy lay and started digging. After a few minutes a villager came out from his hiding spot in the trees and began shouting in Tim's direction, walking fast but with his hands straight above his head so no one would shoot him. Some of the soldiers bristled and put fingers on their triggers, but Tim stuck the shovel in the ground and watched the man come on. He was in his thirties or forties, slender but strong-looking, his shirt soaked through with sweat. He poked himself in the chest repeatedly and said, *Bác*, *bác*.

A couple of the guys had wandered close and stood smoking and watching the man berate Tim.

Harris, what's he saying? Tim asked one of them.

Bác, the man said again.

Means *uncle*, Harris said. Harris had spent three weeks listening to Vietnamese lessons on vinyl at the Reno Public Library before he shipped out. He was shy and cursed with a demanding overbite but had proven himself invaluable again and again, even with such a rudimentary understanding.

Uncle, Tim said.

The man pointed at the E-tool and opened his hand.

No, Harris said. No fucking way.

But when the man moved to pick it up, Tim didn't stop him. The man looked at him and jostled his lips rapidly, praying, conveying some sort of message, before he thrust the spade into the ground. Tim watched him for a minute, the man's sweat dripping into the fresh grave, the little whimper he gave each time he jabbed with the shovel, and without really thinking about it Tim sunk to his knees beside him then and started digging with his bare hands.

With the venom in his veins and the night bent in an arc around him and the trees finally stilled in their twisting he closes his eyes and at last sees his wife. Her shape not now any shape she'd ever taken in the real world; in his mind her shape not so much a body at all but a jumble of color, a skin of variegated dust; when she walks, clouds of it drift away from her limbs like smoke. She crosses his field of vision, a path both simple and preordained, from one darkness into another, as far as his imagination can take her. He begs her to turn around and begin again, but just before she reaches the edge of his periphery she slows and turns her head toward him and her face steadies and shimmers, and he realizes she's calm, though it's quite clear that wherever she is she's caught fire.

❦ ❦ ❦

His mama insisted that he marry Grace. It was never even a question: there was no *Do you think she's the one?* There was no *Plenty of fish in the sea*. Not a matter of love at first sight, as it would seem to be for Anthony and Celia; it was much more deliberate than that, the guiding nature of Grace's affection so obvious to his mama that there was nothing more about the young woman that required her notice. His mama saw in Grace a girl who could keep Tim *alive*, which had nothing to do, of course, with keeping him *happy* or with keeping him *satisfied*. To keep him alive was much more important. Maybe even the only important thing there was.

Put a ring on her finger and get her out of these hills, his mama had said.

Why do we need to leave?

Think of how much life there is that ain't in West Virginia, she said. Go see the beach. Take that little girl to Italy. Eat stuff you haven't never tasted before.

He watched his mama smoking, leaning back in her chair, looking up the hill and wondering what the things she'd never eaten might have tasted like.

I intend to marry her, he said. I've always intended to marry her.

You do that, then, she said. You do that, and afterward you make sure she knows why you done it. Every single day. Don't let a single day go by that she don't know why you picked her. You bring her over here sometimes and I'll tell her why myself.

Okay, Mama.

I'm not playing.

I know it, Mama.

❦ ❦ ❦

Grace is built of a million pixels, and while she burns, frayed clumps of them slip away from her body and disappear into an ether outside his field of vision. She is fading, crumbling, a sandcastle eaten away by the sea. Before her arms are gone she lifts one of them and waves; before her legs go she hikes the blurry hem of her skirt and does a quick dance—the same little soft-shoe she'd done on the parlor hardwood at the cut. Then the dust of her ankles blows away, and the dust of her toes, and before he's ready to say goodbye the entire remnant of her is gone from the whitewashed background of his mind and he is awake.

❧ ❧ ❧

Anthony was drunk and didn't know what he was talking about, but he was adamant that every living person was actually two people mashed into a single body.

Like Siamese twins? Tim said.

They'd finished the last of the whiskey and Anthony had chucked the bottle into the ravine below.

Not like, Anthony said. Jesus. Not like Siamese twins.

Well, Tim said, laughing. What, then?

Like you are you, Anthony said, and also someone else. And there's a switch in you, but you can't switch it by yourself. Life has to switch it for you.

His brother was in it, deep into this thought he was having. Totally sincere in his bullshit.

What happens when you get switched? Tim said.

You turn into the other person. Not the person you think you are, but someone different. And there's a catch. When you get switched, you don't actually know it. You still think you're the same old, same old.

You're talking about yourself.

I'm talking about fucking *everybody.*

You're giving me a reason for what you did in the jungle.

Anthony burped and held his fist to his lips, ready to puke, but swallowed it back down. I'm giving you a reason for why *everybody* does *everything.*

Tim sat quiet for a minute. Dad?

Yup.

Mama?

Uh-huh.

Celia?

Anthony looked at him, poked a finger in his face. Not her. She was the only real one.

The night has gone quiet. Jonas is gone. Jonas may never even have been there.

He pushes himself to his knees and sits for a minute, listening. No more voices from the house. Grace is not beyond him in the woods; she's not walking or dancing or drifting away. She is just nothing again. He turns and gathers the pitch-black forest together. The crickets and cicadas gone quiet. Even the wind is still. Everything is nothing again.

The 1911 is the only gun there is, their father always said. His fingers trembling while he ran them over the honeycomb grip, the inset serial number, the cold black metal and its lettering: *United States Property*. He slid the magazine away, popped the rail back and let the chambered round fly out, handed the gun to Anthony who held it across his two palms like a fish he'd caught. It's heavy, isn't it, their father said. Anthony nodded. Their father drinking, drinking. I ever tell you boys the story of the field kraut? They were too nervous to tell him he had; it was safer just to listen again. Couple of months after Omaha Beach we're on our way to the Loire, their father said. We pull up in a little shithole village and set up camp. Get a fire going. Someone finds a bottle of champagne under the floorboards of a house, and a few of us keep it to ourselves. He glanced at his sons, maybe thinking it wasn't something he should be telling them, went on. Anyway, he said. After a while I gotta pinch a loaf, so I wander off behind a house, and I'm standing in front of this great big cornfield that's been all burnt up. The sun going down in the back of it. Beautiful. So I haul my britches down and I'm squatting against the house and just as I'm working one up a German infantryman steps out from behind a rusted tractor out in the field. Starts running at me, got his

Luger aimed right at my nuts. Screaming at me in German, *ina-hina-fina*, like that, but I got my pants around my ankles, there ain't nothing I can do, all I can do is sit down quick and—*crack!*—he fires a round where I used to be, right into the bricks above me. I reach down to my holster and pull this gun out—he taps the gun in Anthony's hands—and level it and take one shot and hit the fucker right in the cheek. Blew his brains out the back of his head. He stops in his tracks and stands there for a minute, looking at me like *what the hell just happened?*, and then he drops. Their father took the gun from Anthony and put the stray bullet back in the magazine and slid the magazine back in and laid the gun on the table in front of him. You aim this gun at the broad side of a barn, he said, you'll hit the farmer standing there right smack in the throat. And that's why the 1911 is the only gun there is.

❧ ❧ ❧

He walks in the direction he thinks he'd been running. Tripping over roots and bramble, arms out ahead of himself, eyes wide to bring in more moonlight. He squeezes the meat of his thumb, remembering, but it doesn't hurt yet; his hands, like his feet, like his whole body, are numb.

A few minutes later he's standing again in Wiley and Catherine's yard. The house looks different; the lights off, the candles unlit. The house's hulking black shadow pressed into the trees like a terrified child with her back against a wall. He crosses to the porch quietly, knowing already that no one is there, that they must have gone out to search for him, and walks through a mass of cobwebs that cling to his beard and eyebrows. The house emanating a smell of rot. Its porch sagging into the ground like the face of an old man.

Hello, he calls. Presses his face against a window, but sees nothing: the glass is coated with green algae and filth. Everything still. It's as though no one has ever lived there, as though the house had been built for some pioneering young family who never even bothered to move in.

Sunset

FOR A WHILE THE TWO BROTHERS—on the cusp of manhood themselves, though they couldn't have known it—watched the squirrels arguing in the trees, dropping shit on their father's casket and scrabbling across branches like maniacs. The boys laughed and poked each other in the ribs while the preacher said his part, thinking their mother couldn't hear them, though of course she could. Everybody could, and everybody was looking; the poor children had up and lost it. But it was only that something funny was happening, and they'd not yet discovered that there are some places where good spirits are not to make an appearance.

In the evening Anthony stole a bowl of chocolate candy from their grandmother's table and the two of them sat on the front porch and ate all of it, watching the sun go down.

You're gonna be okay? Anthony said.

In fact Tim could think of several ways he'd be *better* than okay now. He hoped his father had found peace, but doubted greatly that he'd miss him. He hoped his mother would find peace, too, and in whatever childish way he could he intended to help her. He thought maybe the pain of watching someone slide, one cool metal can at a time, to the bottom of the ocean, the pain of his not having the strength to pull his father back up, might ease now that Philip was gone.

I'll get used to it, he said.

He takes the dirt road from Wiley and Catherine's back to the trailer, listening for their voices and footsteps, but the woods are dead quiet, as though they've been vacant forever. Passes the Ford, its busted engine and dark cab, the shadows cast into it, light from the moon through the trees like a man vaguely situated inside. He brushes the door with his fingertips as he walks past.

The trailer is as lonely as ever. The grass higher than he'd realized: in just a few short days the path to the creek has nearly been overgrown. He pulls himself onto the stoop and tries to open the door but it's locked. Goes to reach into the busted window panel but it's been replaced.

❧ ❧ ❧

How'd he get his finger chopped off?

Thresher mishap. He was only thirteen or fourteen.

They sat with their legs hanging over the rock and their toes in the creekwater. The sky around them purple and orange. Old Man John in the yard across from them, grazing.

He was trying to unsnarl a belt, she said, and when it caught, it pulled his arm into the flywheel. Heard a snap, felt some pain, pulled his arm out in time to not sever the whole thing, and all that came back missing was his right index finger. Clean slice.

How long did it take to grow a new finger? Tim was humoring her, letting her tell her stories. Helping her stay in touch with her heritage.

He never grew a new finger. I told you. He grew a tail where his finger used to be.

He smiled. Like an actual tail?

Yeah. She laughed like she couldn't believe he was bothering to question it.

Like on a salamander.

Yes, Tim.

What color was it?

Granny Lea says it was greenish.

Greenish.

Yeah.

And what else about it?

Well, look, she said, and held her index finger out. See how mine moves at the joints? It can't but wiggle a little side-to-side, it doesn't go backward, and there's only three places it can bend. She demonstrates each movement with total sincerity.

I see it.

But Crane Patchett's new finger didn't have knuckles like that. Knuckles help it move one way but keep it from moving another. Crane Patchett's new finger, Granny Lea said, moved like a tall piece of grass, any which way it pleased.

He smiled again and looked out over the creek. And just how long did this take to happen?

Oh, a few days, I'd guess.

❦ ❦ ❦

He looks through the front windows but can't see much. Walks around the back and listens—for movement, snoring, the shuffling static sound of life being undertaken quietly. Nothing. Goes back to the stoop and punches out the same panel he'd punched out that first night, unlocks the door from the inside, pushes it open and stands there. The smell different than he remembered; what before had been rot is now just dust, oldness, pleasant in the way of a box of antique books. He steps inside and everything is wrong. The kitchen on the opposite end of the house, the bedroom switched. The mattress is not in the floor and there is no television set at all. No buckshot holes in the wall for the moonlight to seep through. He's confused enough to feel angry.

The dark room moves and shifts. His skull like a bowl of water. He feels himself tilting, catches himself on the wall, leans into it and tries to breathe. He looks down at his thumb but there is still no pain, and all of a sudden what he wants more than anything in the world is a few minutes of sleep. His eyelids have grown heavy, his head dull and full, and his cheek has begun to pulse with fresh hurt, as though someone he can't see is slapping him.

Outside, it's beginning to rain.

❧ ❧ ❧

Maksik sat smoking with Ocasio's body at his feet. The early morning sun had given way to high afternoon heat, and the big soldier had sweat through his t-shirt: his hair drenched, his fingers wetting the pinched end of his smoke. Rivers of sweat down his temples and forehead, some of it dripping onto Ocasio's chest, but the man was dead; he wouldn't care.

The huey they'd called in was long in coming. God knew the reason; it was just the way of the jungle. There were stories of napalm dropped twenty-four hours after a firefight was over. Nothing left to cook but spent cartridges and the bodies of fallen Charlie, already sunken into boot-trampled mud.

He sat at the flap of his hooch and watched Maksik most of the day, the clouds of smoke that hung at his head, the dried lines of salt across his back like shifting dunes. Another man would have wrapped the body in canvas and left it somewhere close by, but what Maksik was doing was somehow braver, and more animal: to him, Ocasio deserved to be seen too, deserved not to be alone in his hour of leaving.

It was supper before the huey crew landed in the field at Maksik's feet. He grunted and rubbed his cigarette out and took up Ocasio's legs while Tim and the rest of the platoon came from wherever else they'd been to help lift, but so many men were unnecessary. Maksik and the huey pilot did most of the work. The others grabbed at Ocasio's clothes, touched his dead legs and his blue skin just long enough that when they got home, they could tell their fathers and drinking buddies that they'd helped load him in, that in *their* platoon, nobody got left behind.

❧ ❧ ❧

His father's duffel is missing. Possibly stolen, though enough is odd, it could be he set it in some disappearing room and forgot; just as likely he ate it, or buried it in the back yard. Enough of this. He steps out onto the grass and stands still, lets the night swirl around him. He draws the 1911 from his waistband and backtracks down the long driveway. He will get in the truck and crank it until it starts. It's had time to charge; it might work. He'll go home, back down to the cut, sleep for days and days and then gather up the pieces of his life and pick out the ones that still fit and jam them back together into something he might someday recognize. He'll do Grace's honor by finishing out the old farm house, do it by thinking of her every day, by never touching another woman, by keeping in close with her parents. She'd been right all along about this. Joining her a foolish idea. The ludicrous thought that a man could bend God's will.

He walks slowly, heavily, propelled not by strength but by the gentle wind at his back. By the time he makes the truck he's nearly asleep. He opens the passenger door and makes to lie across the bench, but his father's duffel sits there in the way, just as he'd set it when he'd first left out of the cut. Just as he'd left it on the drive up. He crosses to the driver's side and pops it open. The cab of the truck smells horribly of shit and rotted meat. He covers his nose and mouth with his t-shirt and climbs in anyway.

The last time he saw his mama was at the funeral. In the days after Grace died he hadn't tried to get in touch but stayed instead with Grace's folks in an angry attempt to drink her smell out of their walls. When that hadn't worked, of course, there had been regret: that he'd drunk instead from Grace's old man's wine, had been drunk, in fact, for days; that he'd not returned to sleep in his boyhood bed to find some solace in going back home again.

His mama understood keenly those things she didn't understand. I tried to bring us to God, she said. They were the center of a swirl of people, each of whom had something to say on their way past, but none of whom lingered.

Mama, that was years ago.

Still.

Can we go outside for a minute?

The funeral home was a cinderblock building painted white. Its parking lot recently redone. She followed him to the back and they sat on a low wall beside the trash cans, smoking cigarettes.

I'd never seen such a reaction to a little book as you boys gave me that time, his mama said. You'd think I'd raised a couple of wolves.

You *did* raise a couple of wolves.

Or that you were raised by wolves yourselves.

It takes one to have the other.

Anthony stumbled out from a service door then and stood looking at them, his back to an enormous orange sunset and the rest of him cast in shadow. He was unsteady, antsy. Clearly drunk.

They're trying to find you, he said.

Who is? Tim said.

Like everybody.

Tell them to fuck off.

All of them?

All of them.

Anthony nodded. I can do that, he said, and stumbled back inside.

He rests his head against the window and lets his mouth hang open, his breathing noisy and wet, tries to cough out a wad of phlegm but only raises a pain in the throat. His father's 1911 beside him on the bench. He can't focus on anything.

From far away, he can hear a girl shouting. Mister, mister, she says. Hey mister. Mister.

The pain in his cheek comes quick, like a snake striking in rhythm: *Pap. Pap. Pap.*

Hey mister, the girl says. Wake up. Then he hears her say, Lord help him.

He can hear the heavy pounding of rain on the hood of the truck, like the first seconds of diving underwater. The sucking sounds in the back of his mouth. The roll of thunder like stones down a hillside. He realizes then that he's stopped breathing and can't remember when that happened.

A man's muffled voice says, LeighAnn. Get away from there, LeighAnn.

I don't know what to do, the girl LeighAnn says. Mister, please. I don't know what to do, and he thinks, before he stops thinking altogether, it's a voice he could listen to for the rest of his life.

Acknowledgments

Lots of people played a role in my becoming a writer, some directly and some inadvertantly. Most of them know who they are.

That said, I owe a sincere debt of gratitude to Dave King, Elisa Albert, Rone Shavers, Ed Schwarzschild, Josh Gesner, Sharon MacNeil, Amber Jackson, and Jennifer Austin.

Elizabeth Puotinen has given me more than I could ever deserve. Her patience and encouragement breathed life into my working days. If this book is a success, it's a success because of her.

My daughter, Penelope, told me I could do anything except fly. I'm not yet sure if she was right, but I'm also not so sure she was wrong.

About the Author

Josh Patrick Sheridan grew up in the Appalachian Mountains of West Virginia and now lives with his family in upstate New York. He teaches at the State University of New York at Albany.

CPSIA information can be obtained
at www.ICGtesting.com
Printed in the USA
LVHW041648081121
702781LV00016B/2711

9 781953 932075